# [RETURN]

"Tell me about our baby," he said. "Was it a boy or a girl?"

"I can't tell you about our child," Mary said.

"Why?"

"I died when it was born."

**SHOCK III**

**RICHARD MATHESON**

*Berkley Books by Richard Matheson*

I AM LEGEND
SHOCK I
SHOCK II
SHOCK III
THE SHORES OF SPACE
THE SHRINKING MAN
A STIR OF ECHOES
WHAT DREAMS MAY COME

# RICHARD MATHESON

## SHOCK III

A BERKLEY BOOK
published by
BERKLEY PUBLISHING CORPORATION

SHOCK III

A Berkley Book / published by arrangement with
the author

PRINTING HISTORY
Dell edition published 1966
Berkley edition / September 1979


For information address: Berkley Publishing Corporation,
200 Madison Avenue, New York, New York 10016.

ISBN: 0-425-04209-X

A BERKLEY BOOK ® TM 757,375

PRINTED IN THE UNITED STATES OF AMERICA

## ACKNOWLEDGMENTS

GIRL OF MY DREAMS, 'TIS THE SEASON TO BE JELLY and THE JAZZ MACHINE originally appeared in *The Magazine of Fantasy and Science Fiction*. Copyright © Mercury Press, Inc. 1963.

THE DISINHERITORS originally appeared in *Fantastic Story Magazine*. Copyright © Best Books, Inc. 1952.

WITCH WAR and MISS STARDUST originally appeared in *Startling Stories*. Copyright © Better Publications 1951 and 1955.

FIRST ANNIVERSARY originally appeared in *Playboy*. Copyright © HMH Publishing Co. Inc. 1960.

FULL CIRCLE originally appeared in *Fantastic Universe*. Copyright © King Size Publications 1953.

NIGHTMARE AT 20,000 FEET was originally published in *Alone by Night* in Ballantine Books. Copyright © Richard Matheson 1961.

SLAUGHTER HOUSE Copyright © *Weird Tales* 1953.

RETURN originally appeared in *Thrilling Wonder Stories*. Copyright © Standard Magazines, Inc. 1951.

WHEN THE WAKER SLEEPS originally appeared under the title THE WAKER DREAMS in *Galaxy*. Copyright © Galaxy Publishing Corporation 1950.

SHOCK WAVE originally appeared in *Gamma*. Copyright © Star Press, Inc. 1963.

# Contents

# Girl of My Dreams

He woke up, grinning, in the darkness. Carrie was having a nightmare. He lay on his side and listened to her breathless moaning. Must be a good one, he thought. He reached out and touched her back. The nightgown was wet with her perspiration. Great, he thought. He pulled his hand away as she squirmed against it, starting to make faint noises in her throat; it sounded as if she were trying to say "No."

No, hell, Greg thought. Dream, you ugly bitch; what else are you good for? He yawned and pulled his left arm from beneath the covers. Three-sixteen. He wound the watch stem sluggishly. Going to get me one of those electric watches one of these days, he thought. Maybe this dream would do it. Too bad Carrie had no control over them. If she did, he could really make it big.

He rolled onto his back. The nightmare was ending now; or coming to its peak, he was never sure which. What difference did it make anyway? He wasn't interested in the machinery, just the product. He grinned again, reaching over to the bedside table for his cigarettes. Lighting one, he blew up smoke. Now he'd have to comfort her, he thought with a frown. That was the part he could live without. Dumb little creep. Why couldn't she be blonde and beautiful? He expelled a burst of smoke. Well, you couldn't ask for everything. If she were good-looking, she probaby wouldn't have these dreams. There were plenty of other women to provide the rest of it.

Carrie jerked violently and sat up with a cry, pulling the covers from his legs. Greg looked at her outline in the darkness. She was shivering. "Oh, no," she whispered. He watched her head begin to shake. "No. No." She started to cry, her body hitching with sobs. Oh, Christ, he thought, this'll take hours. Irritably, he pressed his cigarette into the ashtray and sat up.

"Baby?" he said.

She twisted around with a gasp and stared at him. "Come 'ere," he told her. He opened his arms and she flung herself against him. He could feel her narrow fingers gouging at his back, the soggy weight of her breasts against his chest. Oh, boy, he thought. He kissed her neck, grimacing at the smell of her sweat-damp skin. Oh, boy, what I go through. He caressed her back. "Take it easy, baby," he said, "I'm here." He let her cling to him, sobbing weakly. "Bad dream?" he asked. He tried to sound concerned.

"Oh, Greg." She could barely speak. "It was horrible, oh, God, how horrible."

He grinned. It *was* a good one.

"Which way?" he asked.

Carrie perched stiffly on the edge of the seat, looking through the windshield with troubled eyes. Any second now, she'd pretend she didn't know; she always did. Greg's fingers tightened slowly on the wheel. One of these days, by God, he'd smack her right across her ugly face and walk out, free. Damn freak. He felt the skin begin to tighten across his cheeks. "Well?" he asked.

"I don't—"

"*Which way, Carrie?*" God, he'd like to twist back one of her scrawny arms and break the damn thing; squeeze that skinny neck until her breath stopped.

Carrie swallowed dryly. "Left," she murmured.

Bingo! Greg almost laughed aloud, slapping down the turn indicator. *Left*—right into the Eastridge area, the money area. You dreamed it right this time, you dog, he thought; this is It. All he had to do now was play it smart and he'd be free of her for good. He'd sweated it out and now it was payday!

The tires made a crisp sound on the pavement as he turned

the car onto the quiet, tree-lined street. "How far?" he asked. She didn't answer and he looked at her threateningly. Her eyes were shut.

"How far? I said."

Carrie clutched her hands together. "Greg, please—" she started. Tears were squeezing out beneath her lids.

"Damn it!"

Carrie whimpered and said something. "What?" he snapped. She drew in wavering breath. "The middle of the next block," she said.

"Which side?"

"The right."

Greg smiled. He leaned back against the seat and relaxed. That was more like it. Dumb bitch tried the same old I-forget routine every time. When would she learn that he had her down cold? He almost chuckled. She never would, he thought; because, after this one, he'd be gone and she could dream for nothing.

"Tell me when we reach it," he said.

"Yes," she answered. She had turned her face to the window and was leaning her forehead against the cold glass. Don't cool it too much, he thought, amused; keep it hot for Daddy. He pressed away the rising smile as she turned to look at him. Was she picking up on him? Or was it just the usual? It was always the same. Just before they reached wherever they were going, she'd look at him intently as if to convince herself that it was worth the pain. He felt like laughing in her face. Obviously, it was worth it. How else could a beast like her land someone with his class? Except for him, her bed would be the emptiest, her nights the longest.

"Almost there?" he asked.

Carrie looked to the front again. "The white one," she said.

"With the half-circle drive?"

She nodded tightly. "Yes."

Greg clenched his teeth, a spasm of avidity sweeping through him. Fifty thousand if it was worth a nickel, he thought. Oh, you bitch, you crazy bitch, you really nailed it for me this time! He turned the wheel and pulled in at the curb. Cutting the engine, he glanced across the street. The convertible would come from that direction, he thought. He wondered who'd be driving it. Not that it mattered.

"Greg?"

He turned and eyed her coldly. "What?"

She bit her lip, then started to speak.

"*No*," he said, cutting her off. He pulled out the ignition key and shoved open the door. "Let's go," he said. He slid out, shut the door and walked around the car. Carrie was still inside. "Let's *go*, baby," he said, the hint of venom in his voice.

"Greg, please—"

He shuddered at the cost of repressing an intense desire to scream curses at her, jerk open the door and drag her out by her hair. His rigid fingers clamped on the handle and he opened the door, waited. Christ, but she was ugly—the features, the skin, the body. She'd never looked so repugnant to him. "*I said let's go*," he told her. He couldn't disguise the tremble of fury in his voice.

Carrie got out and he shut the door. It was getting colder. Greg drew up the collar of his topcoat, shivering as they started up the drive toward the front door of the house. He could use a heavier coat, he thought; with a nice, thick lining. A real sharp one, maybe black. He'd get one one of these days—and maybe real soon too. He glanced at Carrie, wondering if she had any notion of his plans. He doubted it even though she looked more worried than ever. What the hell was with her? She'd never been this bad before. Was it because it was a kid? He shrugged. What difference did it make? She'd perform.

"Cheer up," he said. "It's a school day. You won't have to see him." She didn't answer.

They went up two steps onto the brick porch and stopped before the door. Greg pushed the button and, deep inside the house, melodic chimes sounded. While they waited, he reached inside his topcoat pocket and touched the small leather notebook. Funny how he always felt like some kind of weird salesman when they were operating. A salesman with a damned closed market, he thought, amused. No one else could offer what he had to sell, that was for sure.

He glanced at Carrie. "Cheer *up*," he told her. "We're helping them, aren't we?"

Carrie shivered. "It won't be too much, will it, Greg?"

"I'll decide on—"

He broke off as the door was opened. For a moment, he felt angry disappointment that the bell had not been answered by a maid. Then he thought: Oh, what the hell, the money's still here—and he smiled at the woman who stood before them. "Good afternoon," he said.

The woman looked at him with that half polite, half suspicious smile most women gave him at first. "Yes?" she asked.

"It's about Paul," he said.

The smile disappeared, the woman's face grew blank. "What?" she asked.

"That's your son's name, isn't it?"

The woman glanced at Carrie. Already, she was disconcerted, Greg could see.

"He's in danger of his life," he told her. "Are you interested in hearing more about it?"

"*What's happened to him?*"

Greg smiled affably. "Nothing yet," he answered. The woman caught her breath as if, abruptly, she were being strangled.

"You've taken him," she murmured.

Greg's smile broadened. "Nothing like that," he said.

"Where is he then?" the woman asked.

Greg looked at his wristwatch, feigning surprise. "Isn't he at school?" he asked.

Uneasily confused, the woman stared at him for several moments before she twisted away, pushing at the door. Greg caught hold of it before it shut. "Inside," he ordered.

"Can't we wait out—?"

Carrie broke off with a gasp as he clamped his fingers on her arm and pulled her into the hall. While he shut the door,

Greg listened to the rapid whir and click of a telephone being dialed in the kitchen. He smiled and took hold of Carrie's arm again, guiding her into the living room. ''Sit,'' he told her.

Carrie settled gingerly on the edge of a chair while he appraised the room. Money was in evidence wherever he looked, in the carpeting and drapes, the period furniture, the accessories. Greg pulled in a tight, exultant breath and tried to keep from grinning like an eager kid; this was It all right. Dropping onto the sofa, he stretched luxuriously, leaned back and crossed his legs, glancing at the name on a magazine lying on the end table beside him. In the kitchen, he could hear the woman saying, ''He's in Room Fourteen; Mrs. Jennings' class.''

A sudden clicking sound made Carrie gasp. Greg turned his head and saw, through the back drapes, a collie scratching at the sliding glass door; beyond, he noted, with renewed pleasure, the glint of swimming pool water. Greg watched the dog. It must be the one that would—

''*Thank* you,'' said the woman gratefully. Greg turned back and looked in that direction. The woman hung up the telephone receiver and her footsteps tapped across the kitchen floor, becoming soundless as she stepped onto the hallway carpeting. She started cautiously toward the front door.

''We're in here, Mrs. Wheeler,'' said Greg.

The woman caught her breath and whirled in shock. ''What *is* this?'' she demanded.

''Is he all right?'' Greg asked.

''*What do you want?*''

Greg drew the notebook from his pocket and held it out. ''Would you like to look at this?'' he asked.

The woman didn't answer but peered at Greg through narrowing eyes. ''That's right,'' he said. ''We're selling something.''

The woman's face grew hard.

''*Your son's life,*'' Greg completed.

The woman gaped at him, momentary resentment invaded by fear again. Jesus, you look stupid, Greg felt like telling her. He forced a smile. "Are you interested?" he asked.

"Get out of here before I call the police." The woman's voice was husky, tremulous.

"You're not interested in your son's life then?"

The woman shivered with fear-ridden anger. "Did you hear me?" she said.

Greg exhaled through clenching teeth.

"Mrs. Wheeler," he said, "unless you listen to us—*carefully*—your son will soon be dead." From the corners of his eyes, he noticed Carrie wincing and felt like smashing in her face. That's right, he thought with savage fury. Show her how scared you are, you stupid bitch!

Mrs. Wheeler's lips stirred falteringly as she stared at Greg. "What are you talking about?" she finally asked.

"Your son's life, Mrs. Wheeler."

"Why should you want to hurt my boy?" the woman asked, a sudden quaver in her voice. Greg felt himself relax. She was almost in the bag.

"Did I say that we were going to hurt him?" he asked, smiling at her quizzically. "I don't remember saying that, Mrs. Wheeler."

"Then—?"

"Sometime before the middle of the month," Greg interrupted, "Paul will be run over by a car and killed."

"What?"

Greg did not repeat.

"What car?" asked the woman. She looked at Greg in panic. "What car?" she demanded.

"We don't know exactly."

"Where?" the woman asked. "When?"

"That information," Greg replied, "is what we're selling."

The woman turned to Carrie, looking at her frightenedly. Carrie lowered her gaze, teeth digging at her lower lip. The woman looked back at Greg as he continued.

"Let me explain," he said. "My wife is what's known as a 'sensitive.' You may not be familiar with the term. It means she has visions and dreams. Very often, they have to do with real people. Like the dream she had last night—about your son."

The woman shrank from his words and, as Greg expected, an element of shrewdness modified her expression; there was now, in addition to fear, suspicion.

"I know what you're thinking," he informed her. "Don't waste your time. Look at this notebook and you'll see—"

"Get out of here," the woman said.

Greg's smile grew strained. "That again?" he asked. "You mean you really don't care about your son's life?"

The woman managed a smile of contempt. "Shall I call the police now?" she asked. "The *bunco* squad?"

"If you really want to," answered Greg, "but I suggest you listen to me first." He opened the notebook and began to read. "*January twenty-second: Man named Jim to fall from roof while adjusting television aerial. Ramsay Street. Two-story house, green with white trim.* Here's the news item."

Greg glanced at Carrie and nodded once, ignoring her pleading look as he stood and walked across the room. The woman cringed back apprehensively but didn't move. Greg held up the notebook page. "As you can see," he said, "the man didn't believe what we told him and did fall off his roof on January twenty-second; it's harder to convince them when you can't give any details so as not to give it all away." He clucked as if disturbed. "He should have paid us, though," he said. "It would have been a lot less expensive than a broken back."

"Who do you think you're—?"

"Here's another," Greg said, turning a page. "This should interest you. *February twelfth, afternoon: Boy, 13, name unknown, to fall into abandoned well shaft, fracture pelvis. Lives on Darien Circle,* etcetera, etcetera, you can see the details here," he finished, pointing at the page. "Here's the newspaper clipping. As you can see, his parents were just in time. They'd refused to pay at first, threatened to call the police like you did." He smiled at the woman. "Threw us out of the house as a matter of fact," he said. "On the afternoon of the twelfth, though, when I made a last-minute phone check, they were out of their minds with worry. Their son had disappeared and they had no idea where he was—I hadn't mentioned the well shaft, of course."

He paused for a moment of dramatic emphasis, enjoying the moment fully. "I went over to their house," he said. "They made their payment and I told them where their son was." He pointed at the clipping. "He was found, as you see—down in an abandoned well shaft. With a broken pelvis."

"Do you really—?"

"—expect you to believe all this?" Greg completed her thought. "Not completely; no one ever does at first. Let me tell you what you're thinking right now. You're thinking that we cut out these newspaper items and made up this story to fit them. You're entitled to believe that if you want to—" his face hardened, "—but, if you do, you'll have a dead son by the middle of the month, you can count on that."

He smiled cheerfully. "I don't believe you'd enjoy hearing how it's going to happen," he said.

The smile began to fade. "And it *is* going to happen, Mrs. Wheeler, whether you believe it or not."

The woman, still too dazed by fright to be completely sure of her suspicion, watched Greg as he turned to Carrie. "Well?" he said.

"I don't—"

"*Let's have it,*" he demanded.

Carrie bit her lower lip and tried to restrain the sob.

"What are you going to do?" the woman asked.

Greg turned to her with a smile. "Make our point," he said. He looked at Carrie again. "*Well*?"

She answered, eyes closed, voice pained and feeble. "There's a throw rug by the nursery door," she said. "You'll slip on it while you're carrying the baby."

Greg glanced at her in pleased surprise; he hadn't known there was a baby. Quickly, he looked at the woman as Carrie continued in a troubled voice, "There's a black widow spider underneath the playpen on the patio, it will bite the baby, there's a—"

"Care to check these items, Mrs. Wheeler?" Greg broke in. Suddenly, he hated her for her slowness, for her failure to accept. "Or shall we just walk out of here," he said, sharply, "*and let that blue convertible drag Paul's head along the street until his brains spill out?*"

The woman looked at him in horror. Greg felt a momentary dread that he had told her too much, then relaxed as he realized that he hadn't. "I suggest you check," he told her, pleasantly. The woman backed away from him a little bit, then turned and hurried toward the patio door. "Oh, incidentally," Greg said, remembering. She turned. "That dog out there will try to save your son but it won't succeed; the car will kill it, too."

The woman stared at him, as if uncomprehending, then turned away and, sliding open the patio door, went outside. Greg saw the collie frisking around her as she moved across the patio. Leisurely, he returned to the sofa and sat down.

"Greg—?"

He frowned grimacingly, jerking up his hand to silence her. Out on the patio, there was a scraping noise as the woman overturned the playpen. He listened intently. There was a sudden gasp, then the stamping of the woman's shoe on concrete, an excited barking by the dog. Greg smiled and leaned back with a sigh. Bingo.

When the woman came back in, he smiled at her, noticing how heavily she breathed.

"That could happen any place," she said, defensively.

"Could it?" Greg's smile remained intact. "And the throw rug?"

"Maybe you looked around while I was in the kitchen."

"We didn't."

"*Maybe you guessed.*"

"And maybe we didn't," he told her, chilling his smile. "Maybe everything we've said is true. You want to gamble on it?"

The woman had no reply. Greg looked at Carrie. "Anything else?" he asked. Carrie shivered fitfully. "An electric outlet by the baby's crib," she said. "She has a bobby pin beside her, she's been trying to put it in the plug and—''

''Mrs. Wheeler?'' Greg looked inquisitively at the woman. He snickered as she turned and hurried from the room. When she was gone, he smiled and winked at Carrie. ''You're really on today, baby,'' he said. She returned his look with glistening eyes. ''Greg, please don't make it too much,'' she murmured.

Greg turned away from her, the smile withdrawn. Relax, he told himself; relax. After today, you'll be free of her. Casually, he slipped the notebook back into his topcoat pocket.

The woman returned in several minutes, her expression now devoid of anything but dread. Between two fingers of her right hand she was carrying a bobby pin. ''*How did you know*?'' she asked. Her voice was hollow with dismay.

''I believe I explained that, Mrs. Wheeler,'' Greg replied. ''My wife has a gift. She knows exactly where and when the accident will occur. Do you care to buy that information?''

The woman's hands twitched at her sides. ''What do you want?'' she asked.

''Ten thousand dollars in cash,'' Greg answered. His fingers flexed reactively as Carrie gasped but he didn't look at her. He fixed his gaze on the woman's stricken face. ''Ten thousand . . .'' she repeated dumbly.

''That's correct. Is it a deal?''

''But we don't—''

''*Take it or leave it, Mrs. Wheeler*. You're not in a bargaining position. Don't think for a second that there's anything you can do to prevent the accident. Unless you know the exact time and place, it's going to happen.'' He stood abruptly, causing her to start. ''Well?'' he snapped, ''what's it going to be? Ten thousand dollars or your son's life?''

The woman couldn't answer. Greg's eyes flicked to where Carrie sat in mute despair. ''Let's go,'' he said. He started for the hall.

''*Wait*.''

Greg turned and looked at the woman. ''Yes?''

''How—do I know—?'' she faltered.

"You don't," he broke in; "you don't know a thing. *We* do."

He waited another few moments for her decision, then walked into the kitchen and, removing his memo pad from an inside pocket, slipped the pencil free and jotted down the telephone number. He heard the woman murmuring pleadingly to Carrie and, shoving the pad and pencil into his topcoat pocket, left the kitchen. "Let's go," he said to Carrie who was standing now. He glanced disinterestedly at the woman. "I'll phone this afternoon," he said. "You can tell me then what you and your husband have decided to do." His mouth went hard. "*It'll be the only call you'll get*," he said.

He turned and walked to the front door, opened it. "Come on, come on," he ordered irritably. Carrie slipped by him, brushing at the tears on her cheeks. Greg followed and began to close the door, then stopped as if remembering something.

"Incidentally," he said. He smiled at the woman. "I wouldn't call the police if I were you. There's nothing they could charge us with even if they found us. And, of course, we couldn't tell you then—and your son would have to die." He closed the door and started for the car, a picture of the woman printed in his mind: standing, dazed and trembling, in her living room, looking at him with haunted eyes. Greg grunted in amusement.

She was hooked.

Greg drained his glass and fell back heavily on the sofa arm, making a face. It was the last cheap whiskey he'd ever drink; from now on, it was exclusively the best. He turned his head to look at Carrie. She was standing by the window of their hotel living room, staring at the city. What the hell was she brooding about now? Likely, she was wondering where that blue convertible was. Momentarily, Greg wondered himself. Was it parked?—moving? He grinned drunkenly. It gave him a feeling of power to know something about that car that even its owner didn't know: namely, that, in eight days, at two-sixteen on a Thursday afternoon, it would run down a little boy and kill him.

He focused his eyes and glared at Carrie. "All right, say it," he demanded. "Get it out."

She turned and looked at him imploringly. "Does it have to be so much?" she asked.

He turned his face away from her and closed his eyes.

"Greg, does it—"

"*Yes*!" He drew in shaking breath. God, would he be glad to get away from her!

"What if they can't pay?"

"*Tough*."

The sound of her repressed sob set his teeth on edge. "Go in and lie down," he told her.

"Greg, he hasn't got a chance!"

He twisted around, face whitening. "Did he have a better chance before we came?" he snarled. "Use your head for once, God damn it! If it wasn't for us, he'd be as good as dead already!"

"Yes, but—"

"I said go in and lie down!"

"You haven't seen the way it's going to happen, Greg!"

He shuddered violently, fighting back the urge to grab the whiskey bottle, leap at her and smash her head in. "*Get out of here*," he muttered.

She stumbled across the room, pressing the back of a hand against her lips. The bedroom door thumped shut and he heard her fall across the bed, sobbing. Damn wet-eye bitch! He gritted his teeth until his jaws hurt, then poured himself another inch of whiskey, grimacing as it burned its way into his stomach. They'll come through, he told himself. Obviously, they had the money and, obviously, the woman had believed him. He nodded to himself. They'll come through, all right. Ten thousand; his passport to another life. Expensive clothes. A class hotel. Good-looking women; maybe one of them for keeps. He kept nodding. One of these days, he thought.

He was reaching for his glass when he heard the muffled sound of Carrie talking in the bedroom. For several moments, his outstretched hand hovered between the sofa and the table. Then, in an instant, he was on his feet, lunging for the bedroom door. He flung it open. Carrie jerked around, the phone receiver in her hand, her face a mask of dread. "Thursday, the fourteenth!" she blurted into the mouthpiece. "Two-sixteen in the afternoon!" She screamed as Greg wrenched the receiver from her hand and slammed his palm on the cradle, breaking the connection.

He stood quivering before her, staring at her face with widened, maniac eyes. Slowly, Carrie raised her hand to avert the blow. "Greg, please don't—" she began.

Fury deafened him. He couldn't hear the heavy, thudding sound the earpiece made against her cheek as he slammed it across her face with all his might. She fell back with a strangled cry. "You bitch," he gasped. "You bitch, you bitch, you bitch!" He emphasized each repetition of the word with another savage blow across her face. He couldn't see her clearly either; she kept wavering behind a film of blinding rage. Everything was finished! She'd blown the deal! The Big One was gone! *God damn it, I'll kill you!* He wasn't certain if the words exploded in his mind or if he was shouting them into her face.

Abruptly, he became aware of the telephone receiver clutched in his aching hand; of Carrie lying, open-mouthed and staring on the bed, her features mashed and bloody. He lost his grip and heard, as if it were a hundred miles below, the receiver thumping on the floor. He stared at Carrie, sick with horror. Was she dead? He pressed his ear against her chest and listened. At first, he could hear only the pulse of his own heart throbbing in his ears. Then, as he concentrated, his expression tautly rabid, he became aware of Carrie's heartbeat, faint and staggering. She wasn't dead! He jerked his head up.

She was looking at him, mouth slack, eyes dumbly stark.

"Carrie?"

No reply. Her lips moved soundlessly. She kept on staring at him. "What?" he asked. He recognized the look and shuddered. "*What*?"

"Street," she whispered.

Greg bent over, staring at her mangled features. "Street," she whispered, ". . . night." She sucked in wheezing, blood-choked breath. "Greg." She tried to sit up but couldn't. Her expression was becoming one of terrified concern. She whispered, "Man . . . razor . . . you—oh, *no*!"

Greg felt himself enveloped in ice. He clutched at her arm. "Where?" he mumbled. She didn't answer and his fingers dug convulsively into her flesh. "Where?" he demanded. "When?" He began to shiver uncontrollably. "Carrie, *when*?!"

It was the arm of a dead woman that he clutched. With a gagging sound, he jerked his hand away. He gaped at her, unable to speak or think. Then, as he backed away, his eyes were drawn to the calendar on the wall and a phrase crept leadenly across his mind: *one of these days*. Quite suddenly, he began to laugh and cry. And before he fled, he stood at the window for an hour and twenty minutes, staring out, wondering who the man was, where he was right now and just what he was doing.

# 'Tis the Season To Be Jelly

Pa's nose fell off at breakfast. It fell right into Ma's coffee and displaced it. Prunella's wheeze blew out the gut lamp.

"Land o' goshen, Dad," Ma said, in the gloom, "if ya know'd it was ready t'plop, whyn't ya tap it off y'self?"

"Didn't know," said Pa.

"That's what ya said the last time, Paw," said Luke, choking on his bark bread. Uncle Rock snapped his fingers beside the lamp. Prunella's wheezing shot the flicker out.

"Shet off ya laughin', gal," scolded Ma. Prunella toppled off her rock in a flurry of stumps, spilling liverwort mush.

"Tarnation take it!" said Uncle Eyes.

"Well, combust the wick, combust the wick!" demanded Grampa, who was reading when the light went out. Prunella wheezed, thrashing on the dirt.

Uncle Rock got sparks again and lit the lamp.

"Where was I now?" said Grampa.

"Git back up here," Ma said. Prunella scrabbled back onto her rock, eye streaming tears of laughter. "Giddy chile," said Ma. She slung another scoop of mush on Prunella's board. "Go to," she said. She picked Pa's nose out of her corn coffee and pitched it at him.

"Ma, I'm fixin' t'ask 'er t'*day*," said Luke.

"Be ya, son?" said Ma. "Thet's nice."

"Ain't no pu'pose to it!" Grampa said. "The dang force o'life is spent!"

"Now, Pa," said Pa, "Don't fuss the young 'uns' mind-to."

"Says right hyeh!" said Grampa, tapping at the journal with his wrist. "We done let in the wavelen'ths of anti-life, that's what we done!"

"*Manure*," said Uncle Eyes. "Ain't we livin'?"

"I'm talkin' 'bout the coming gene-rations, ya dang fool!" Grampa said. He turned to Luke. "Ain't no pu'pose to it, boy!" he said. "You cain't have no young 'uns nohow!"

"Thet's what they tole Pa 'n' me too," soothed Ma, "An' we got two lovely chillun. Don't ya pay no mind t'Grampa, son."

"We's comin' apart!" said Grampa. "Our cells is unlockin'! Man says right hyeh! We's like jelly, breakin'-down jelly!"

"Not me," said Uncle Rock.

"When you fixin' t'ask 'er, son?" asked Ma.

"We done bollixed the pritecktive canopee!" said Grampa.

"Can o' what?" said Uncle Eyes.

"This mawnin'," said Luke.

"We done pregnayted the clouds!" said Grampa.

"She'll be mighty glad," said Ma. She rapped Prunella on the skull with a mallet. "Eat with ya mouth, chile," she said.

"We'll get us hitched up come May," said Luke.

"We done low-pressured the weather sistem!" Grampa said.

"We'll get ya corner ready," said Ma.

Uncle Rock, cheeks flaking, chewed mush.

"We done screwed up the dang master plan!" said Grampa.

"Aw, shet yer ravin' craw!" said Uncle Eyes.

"Shet yer own!" said Grampa.

"Let's have a little ear-blessin' harminy round hyeh," said Pa, scratching his nose. He spat once and downed a flying spider. Prunella won the race.

"Dang leg," said Luke, hobbling back to the table. He

punched the thigh bone back into play. Prunella ate wheezingly.

"Leg aloosenin' agin, son?" asked Ma.

She'll hold, I reckon," said Luke.

"Says right hyeh!" said Grampa, "we'uns clompin' round under a killin' umbrella. A umbrella o'death!"

"*Bull*," said Uncle Eyes. He lifted his middle arm and winked at Ma with the blue one. "Go 'long," said Ma, gumming off a chuckle. The east wall fell in.

"Thar she goes," observed Pa.

Prunella tumbled off her rock and rolled out, wheezing, through the opening. "High-speerited gal," said Ma, brushing cheek flakes off the table.

"What about my corner now?" asked Luke.

"Says right hyeh!" said Grampa, " 'lectric charges is afummadiddled! 'Tomic structure's unseamin'!!"

"We'll prop 'er up again," said Ma. "Don't ya fret none, Luke."

"Have us a wing-ding," said Uncle Eyes. "Jute beer 'n' all."

"Ain't no pu'pose to it!" said Grampa. "We done smithereened the whole kiboodle!"

"Now, Pa," said Ma, "ain't no pu'pose in apreachin' doom nuther. Ain't they been apreachin' it since I was a tyke? Ain't no reason in the wuld why Luke hyeh shouldn't hitch hisself up with Annie Lou. Ain't he got him two strong arms and four strong legs? Ain't no sense in settin' out the dance o' life."

"We'uns ain't got naught t'fear but fear its own self," observed Pa.

Uncle Rock nodded and raked a sulphur match across his jaw to light his punk.

"Ya gotta have faith," said Ma. "Ain't no sense in Godless gloomin' like them signtist fellers."

"Stick 'em in the army, I say," said Uncle Eyes. "Poke a Z-bomb down their britches an' send 'em jiggin' at the enemy!"

"Spray 'em with fire acids," said Pa.

"Stick 'em in a jug o' germ juice," said Uncle Eyes. "Whiff a fog o' vacuum viriss up their snoots. Give 'em hell Columbia."

"That'll teach 'em," Pa observed.

*"We wawked t'gether through*
*the yallar rain.*
*Our luv was stronger than the*
*blisterin' pain*
*The sky was boggy and yer skin*
*was new*
*My hearts was beatin'—Annie,*
*I luv you."*

Luke raced across the mounds, phantomlike in the purple light of his gutbucket. His voice swirled in the soup as he sang the poem he'd made up in the well one day. He turned left at Fallout Ridge, followed Missile Gouge to Shockwave Slope, posted to Radiation Cut and galloped all the way to Mushroom Valley. He wished there were horses. He had to stop three times to reinsert his leg.

Annie Lou's folks were hunkering down to dinner when Luke arrived. Uncle Slow was still eating breakfast.

"Howdy, Mister Mooncalf," said Luke to Annie Lou's pa.

"Howdy, Hoss," said Mr. Mooncalf.

"Pass," said Uncle Slow.

"Draw up sod," said Mr. Mooncalf. "Plenty chow fer all."

"Jest et," said Luke. "Whar's Annie Lou?"

"Out the well fetchin' whater," Mr. Mooncalf said, ladling bitter vetch with his flat hand.

"The," said Uncle Slow.

"Reckon I'll help 'er lug the bucket then," said Luke.

"How's ya folks?" asked Mrs. Mooncalf, salting pulse seeds.

"Jest fine," said Luke. "Top o' the heap."

"Mush," said Uncle Slow.

"Glad t'hear it, Hoss," said Mr. Mooncalf.

"Give 'em our crawlin' best," said Mrs. Mooncalf.

"Sure will," said Luke.

"Dammit," said Uncle Slow.

Luke surfaced through the air hole and cantered toward the well, kicking aside three littles and one big that squished irritably.

"How is yo folks?" asked the middle little.

"None o' yo dang business," said Luke.

Annie Lou was drawing up the water bucket and holding on the side of the well. She had an armful of loose bosk blossoms.

Luke said, "Howdy."

"Howdy, Hoss," she wheezed, flashing her tooth in a smile of love.

"What happened t'yer other ear?" asked Luke.

"Aw, Hoss," she giggled. Her April hair fell down the well. "Aw, pshaw," said Annie Lou.

"Tell ya," said Luke. "Somep'n on my cerebeelum. Got that wud from Grampa," he said, proudly. "Means I got me a mindful."

"That right?" said Annie Lou, pitching bosk blossoms in his face to hide her rising color.

"Yep," said Luke, grinning shyly. He punched at his thigh bone. "Dang leg," he said.

"Givin' ya trouble agin, Hoss?" asked Annie Lou.

"Don't matter none," said Luke. He picked a swimming spider from the bucket and plucked at its legs. "Sh'luvs me," he said, blushing. "Sh'luvs me not. Ow!" The spider flipped away, teeth clicking angrily.

Luke gazed at Annie Lou, looking from eye to eye.

"Well," he said, "will ya?"

"Oh, Hoss!" She embraced him at the shoulders and waist. "I thought you'd never ask!"

"Ya *will?*"

"*Sho!*"

"Creeps!" cried Luke. "I'm the happiest Hoss wot ever lived!"

At which he kissed her hard on the lip and went off racing across the flats, curly mane streaming behind, yelling and whooping.

"Ya-hoo! I'm so happy! I'm so happy, happy, happy!"

His leg fell off. He left it behind, dancing.

# Return

Professor Robert Wade was just sitting down on the thick fragrant grass when he saw his wife Mary come rushing past the Social Sciences Building and onto the campus.

She had apparently run all the way from the house—a good half mile. And with a child in her. Wade clenched his teeth angrily on the stem of his pipe.

Someone had told her.

He could see how flushed and breathless she was as she hurried around the ellipse of walk facing the Liberal Arts Building. He pushed himself up.

Now she was starting down the wide path that paralleled the length of the enormous granite-faced Physical Sciences Center. Her bosom rose and fell rapidly. She raised her right hand and pushed back wisps of dark brown hair.

Wade called, "Mary! Over here!" and gestured with his pipe.

She slowed down, gasping in the cool September air. Her eyes searched over the wide sunlit campus until she saw him. Then she ran off the walk onto the grass. He could see the pitiful fright marring her features and his anger faded. Why did anyone have to tell her?

She threw herself against him. "You said you wouldn't go this time," she said, the words spilling out in gasps. "You said s-someone else would go this time."

"Shhh, darling" he soothed. "Get your breath."

He pulled a handkerchief from his coat pocket and gently

patted her forehead.

"Robert, why?" she asked.

"Who told you?" he asked. "I told them not to."

She pulled back and stared at him. "Not tell me!" she said. "You'd go without telling me?"

"Is it surprising that I don't want you frightened?" he said. "Especially now, with the baby coming?"

"But Robert," she said, "you have to tell me about a thing like that."

"Come on," he said, "let's go over to that bench."

They started across the green, arms around each other.

"You said you wouldn't go," she reminded him.

"Darling, it's my job."

They reached the bench and sat down. He put his arm around her.

"I'll be home for supper," he said. "It's just an afternoon's work."

She looked terrified.

"To go five hundred years into the future!" she cried. "Is that just an afternoon's work?"

"Mary," he said, "you know John Randall has traveled five years and I've traveled a hundred. Why do you start worrying now?"

She closed her eyes. "I'm not just starting," she murmured. "I've been in agony ever since you men intented that—*that thing*."

Her shoulders twitched and she began to cry again. He gave her his handkerchief with a helpless look on his face.

"Listen," he said, "do you think John would let me go if there was any danger? Do you think Doctor Phillips would?"

"But why you?" she asked. "Why not a student?"

"We have no right to send a student, Mary."

She looked out at the campus, plucking at the handkerchief.

"I knew it would be no use talking," she said.

He had no reply.

"Oh, I know it's your job," she said. "I have no right to complain. It's just that—" She turned to him. "Robert, don't lie to me. Will you be in danger. Is there any chance at all that you . . . won't come back?"

He smiled reassuringly. "My dear, there's no more risk than there was the other time. After all it's—" He stopped as she pressed herself against him.

"There'd be no life for me without you," she said. "You know that. I'd die."

"Shhh," he said. "No talk of dying. Remember there are two lives in you now. You've lost your right to private despair." He raised her chin with his hand. "Smile?" he said. "For me? There. That's better. You're much too pretty to cry."

She caressed his hand.

"Who told you?" he asked.

"I'm not snitching," she said with a smile. "Anyway, the one who told me assumed that I already knew."

"Well, now you know," he said. "I'll be back for supper. Simple as that." He started to knock the ashes out of his pipe. "Any errand you'd like me to perform in the twenty-fifth century?" he asked, a smile tugging at the corners of his lean mouth.

"Say hello to Buck Rogers," she said, as he pulled out his watch. Her face grew worried again, and she whispered, "How soon?"

"About forty minutes."

"Forty min—" She grasped his hand and pressed it against her cheek. "You'll come back to me?" she said, looking into his eyes.

"I'll be back," he said, patting her cheek fondly. Then he put on a face of mock severity.

"Unless," he said, "you have something for a supper I don't like."

He was thinking about her as he strapped himself into a sitting position in the dim time-chamber.

The large, gleaming sphere rested on a base of thick

conductors. The air crackled with the operation of giant dynamos.

Through the tall, single-paned windows, sunlight streamed across the rubberized floors like outflung bolts of gold cloth. Students and instructors hurried in and out among the shadows, checking preparing Transposition T-3. On the wall a buzzer sounded ominously.

Everyone on the floor made their final adjustments, then walked quickly to the large, glass-fronted control room and entered.

A short, middle-aged man in a white lab coat came out and strode over to the chamber. He peered into its gloomy interior.

"Bob?" he said. "You want to see me?"

"Yes," Wade said. "I just wanted to say the usual thing. On the vague possibility that I'm unable to return, I—"

"Usual thing!" snorted Professor Randall. "If you think there's any possibility of it at all, get out of that chamber. We're not that interested in the future." He squinted into the chamber. "You smiling?" he asked. "Can't see clearly."

"I'm smiling."

"Good. Nothing to worry about. Just keep strapped in, mind your p's and q's and don't go flirting with any of those Buck Rogers women."

Wade chuckled. "That reminds me," he said. "Mary asked me to say hello to Buck Rogers. Anything you'd like me to do?"

"Just be back in an hour," growled Randall. He reached in and shook hands with Wade. "All strapped?"

"All strapped," Wade answered.

"Good. We'll bounce you out of here in, uh—" Randall looked up at the large red-dialed clock on the firebrick wall. "In eight minutes. Check?"

"Check," Wade said. "Say good-bye to Doctor Phillips for me."

"Will do. Take care, Bob."

"See you."

Wade watched his friend walk back across the floor to the control room. Then, taking a deep breath, he pulled the thick circular door shut and turned the wheel locking it. All sound was cut off.

"Twenty-four seventy-five, here I come," he muttered.

The air seemed heavy and thin. He knew it was only an illusion. He looked quickly at the control board clock. Six minutes. Or five? No matter. He was ready. He rubbed a hand over his brow. Sweat dripped from his palm.

"Hot," he said. His voice was hollow, unreal.

Four minutes.

He let go of the bracing handle with his left hand and, reaching into his back pants pocket, he drew out his wallet. As he opened it to look at Mary's picture, his fingers lost their grip, and the wallet thudded on the metal deck.

He tried to reach it. The straps held him back. He glanced nervously at the clock. Three and a half minutes. Or two and a half? He'd forgotten when John had started the count.

His watch registered a different time. He gritted his teeth. He couldn't leave the wallet there. It might get sucked into the whirring fan and be destroyed and destroy him as well.

Two minutes was time enough.

He fumbled at the waist and chest straps, pulled them open and picked up the wallet. As he started to rebuckle the straps, he squinted once more at the clock. One and a half minutes. Or—

Suddenly the sphere began to vibrate.

Wade felt his muscles contract. The slack waist band snapped open and whipped against the bulkhead. A sudden pain filled his chest and stomach. The wallet fell again.

He grabbed wildly for the bracing handles, exerted all his strength to keep himself pressed to the seat.

He was hurled through the universe. Stars whistled past his ear. A fist of icy fear punched at his heart.

"Mary!" he cried through a tight, fear-bound throat.

Then his head snapped back against the metal. Something exploded in his brain, and he slumped forward. The rushing darkness blotted out consciousness.

It was cool. Pure, exhilarating air washed over the numbed layers of his brain. The touch of it was a pleasant balm to him.

Wade opened his eyes and gazed fixedly at the dull gray ceiling. He twisted his head to follow the drop of the walls. Slight twinges fluttered in his flesh. He winced and moved his head back to its original position.

"Professor Wade."

He started up at the voice, fell back in hissing pain.

"Please remain motionless, Professor Wade," the voice said.

Wade tried to speak but his vocal cords felt numb and heavy.

"Don't try to speak," said the voice. "I'll be in presently."

There was a click, then silence.

Slowly Wade turned his head to the side and looked at the room.

It was about twenty feet square with a fifteen-foot ceiling. The walls and ceiling were of a uniform dullish gray. The floor was black; some sort of tile. In the far wall was the almost invisible outline of a door.

Beside the couch on which he lay was an irregualrly shaped three-legged structure. Wade took it for a chair.

There was nothing else. No other furniture, pictures, rugs, or even source of light. The ceiling seemed to be glowing. Yet, at every spot he concentrated his gaze, the glow faded into lusterless gray.

He lay there trying to recall what had happened. All he could remember was the pain, the flooding tide of blackness.

With considerable pain he rolled onto his right side and got a shaky hand into his rear trouser pocket.

Someone had picked his wallet up from the chamber deck and put it back in his pocket. Stiff-fingered, he drew it out, opened it, and looked at Mary smiling at him from the porch of their home.

The door opened with a gasp of compressed air and a robed man entered.

His age was indeterminate. He was bald, and his wrinkleless features presented an unnatural smoothness like that of an immobile mask.

"Professor Wade," he said.

Wade's tongue moved ineffectively. The man came over to the couch and drew a small plastic box from his robe pocket. Opening it, he took out a small hypodermic and drove it into Wade's arm.

Wade felt a soothing flow of warmth in his veins. It seemed to unknot ligaments and muscles, loosen his throat and activate his brain centers.

"That's better," he said. "Thank you."

"Quite all right," said the man, sitting down on the three-legged structure and sliding the case into his pocket. "I imagine you'd like to know where you are."

"Yes, I would."

"You've reached your goal, Professor—2475—exactly."

"Good. Very good," Wade said. He raised up on one elbow. The pain had disappeared. "My chamber," he said, "is it all right?"

"I dare say," said the man. "It's down in the machine laboratory."

Wade breathed easier. He slid the wallet into his pocket.

"Your wife was a lovely woman," said the man.

"Was?" Wade asked in alarm.

"You didn't think she was going to live five hundred years did you?" said the man.

Wade looked dazed. Then an awkward smile raised his lips.

"It's a little difficult to grasp," he said. "To me she's still alive."

He sat up and put his legs over the edge of the couch.

"I'm Clemolk," said the man. "I'm an historian. You're in the History Pavilion in the city Greenhill."

"United States?"

"Nationalist States," said the historian.

Wade was silent a moment. Then he looked up suddenly and asked, "Say, how long have I been unconscious?"

"You've been 'unconscious,' as you call it, for a little

more than two hours.''

Wade jumped up. ''My God,'' he said anxiously, ''I'll have to leave.''

Clemolk looked at him blandly. ''Nonsense,'' he said. ''Please sit down.''

''But—''

''Please. Let me tell you what you're here for.''

Wade sat down, a puzzled look on his face. A vague uneasiness began to stir in him.

''Here for?'' he muttered.

''Let me show you something,'' Clemolk said.

He drew a small control board from his robe and pushed one of its many buttons.

The walls seemed to fall away. Wade could see the exterior of the building. High up, across the huge entablature were the words: HISTORY IS LIVING. After a moment the wall was there again, solid and opaque.

''Well?'' Wade asked.

''We build our history texts, you see, not on records but on direct testimony.''

''I don't understand.''

''We transcribe the testimony of people who lived in the times we wish to study.''

''But how?''

''By the re-formation of disincarnate personalities.''

Wade was dumbfounded. ''*The dead*?'' he asked hollowly.

''We call them the bodiless,'' replied Clemolk.

''In the natural order, Professor,'' the historian said, ''man's personality exists apart from and independent of his corporeal frame. We have taken this truism and used it to our advantage. Since the personality retains indefinitely—although in decreasing strength—the memory of its physical form and habiliments, it is only a matter of supplying the organic and inorganic materials to this memory.''

''But that's incredible,'' Wade said. ''At Fort—that's the college where I teach—we have psychical research projects.

But nothing approaching this." Suddenly he paled. "Why am *I* here?"

"In your case," Clemolk said, "we were spared the difficulty of re-forming a long bodiless personality from your time period. You reached our period in your chamber."

Wade clasped his shaking hands and blew out a heavy breath.

"This is all very interesting," he said, "but I can't stay long. Suppose you ask me what you want to know."

Clemolk drew out the control board and pushed a button. "Your voice will be transcribed now," he said.

He leaned back and clasped his colorless hands on his lap.

"Your governmental system," he said. "Suppose we start with that."

"Yes," Clemolk said, "it all balances nicely with what we already know."

"Now, may I see my chamber?" Wade asked.

Clemolk's eyes looked at him without flickering. His motionless face was getting on Wade's nerves.

"I think you can *see* it," Clemolk said, getting up.

Wade got up and followed the historian through the doorway into a long similarly shaded and illuminated hall.

You can *see* it.

Wade's brow was twisted into worried lines. Why the emphasis on that word, as though to see the chamber was all he would be allowed to do?

Clemolk seemed unaware of Wade's uneasy thoughts.

"As a scientist," he was saying, "you should be interested in the aspects of re-formation. Every detail is clearly defined. The only difficulty our scientists have yet to cope with is the strength of memory and its effect on the re-formed body. The weaker the memory, you see, the sooner the body disintegrates."

Wade wasn't listening. He was thinking about his wife.

"You see," Clemolk went on, "although, as I said, these disincarnate personalities are re-formed in a vestigial pattern that includes every item to the last detail—including clothes and personal belongings—they last for shorter and shorter periods of time.

'The time allowances vary. A re-formed person, from your period, say, would last about three quarters of an hour."

The historian stopped and motioned Wade toward a door that had opened in the wall of the hallway.

"Here," he said, "we'll take the tube over to the laboratory."

They entered a narrow, dimly lit chamber. Clemolk directed Wade to a wall bench.

The door slid shut quickly and a hum rose in the air. Wade had the immediate sensation of being back in the time-chamber again. He felt the pain, the crushing weight of depression, the wordless terror billowing up in memory.

"Mary." His lips soundlessly formed her name....

The chamber was resting on a broad metal platform. Three men, similar to Clemolk in appearance were examining its exterior surface.

Wade stepped up on the platform and touched the smooth metal with his palms. It comforted him to feel it. It was a tangible link with the past—and his wife.

Then a look of concern crossed his face. Someone had locked the door. He frowned. Opening it from the outside was a difficult and imperfect method.

One of the students spoke. "Will you open it? We didn't want to cut it open."

A pang of fear coursed through Wade. If they had cut it open, he would have been stranded forever.

"I'll open it," he said. "I have to leave now anyway." He said it with forced belligerence, as though he dared them to say otherwise.

The silence that greeted his remark frightened him. He heard Clemolk whisper something.

Pressing his lips together, he began hesitantly to move his fingers over the combination dials.

In his mind, Wade planned quickly, desperately. He

would open the door, jump in and pull it shut behind him before they could make a move.

Clumsily, as if they were receiving only vague direction from his brain, his fingers moved over the thick dials on the center of the door. His lips moved as he repeated to himself the numbers of the combination: 3.2—5.9—7.6—9.01. He paused, then tugged at the handle.

The door would not open.

Drops of perspiration beaded on his forehead and ran down his face. The combination had eluded him.

He struggled to concentrate and remember. He had to remember! Closing his eyes, he leaned against the chamber. Mary, he thought, please help me. Again he fumbled at the dials.

Not 7.6 he suddenly realized. It was 7.8.

His eyes flashed open. He turned the dial to 7.8. The lock was ready to open.

"You'd b-better step back," Wade said, turning to the four men. "There's liable to be an escape of... locked-in gases." He hoped they wouldn't guess how desperately he was lying.

The students and Clemolk stepped back a little. They were still close, but he had to risk it.

Wade jerked open the door and in his plunge through the opening, slipped on the smooth platform surface and crashed down on one knee. Before he could rise, he felt himself grabbed on both sides.

Two students started to drag him off the platform.

"No!" he screamed. "I have to go back!"

He kicked and struggeled, his fists flailed the air. Now the other two men held him back. Tears of rage flew from his eyes as he writhed furiously in their grip, shrieking, "Let me go!"

A sudden pain jabbed Wade's back. He tore away from one student and dragged the others around in a last surge of enraged power. A glimpse of Clemolk showed the historian holding another hypodermic.

Wade would have tired to lunge for him, but on the instant

a complete lassitude watered his limbs. He slumped down on his knees, glassy-eyed, one numbing hand outflung in vain appeal.

"Mary," he muttered hoarsely.

Then he was on his back and Clemolk was standing over him. The historian seemed to waver and disappear before Wade's clouding eyes.

"I'm sorry," Clemolk was saying. "You can't go back—ever."

Wade lay on the couch again, staring at the ceiling and still turning over Clemolk's words in his mind.

"It's impossible that you return. You've been transposed in time. You now belong to this period."

Mary was waiting.

Supper would be on the stove. He could see her setting the table, her slender fingers putting down plates, cups, sparkling glasses, silverware. She'd be wearing a clean, fluffy apron over her dress.

Then the food was ready. She'd be sitting at the table waiting for him. Deep within himself Wade felt the unspoken terror in her mind.

He twisted his head on the couch in agony. Could it possibly be true? Was he really imprisoned five centuries from his rightful existence? It was insane. But he was *here*. The yielding coach was definitely under him, the grey walls around him. Everything was real.

He wanted to surge up and scream, to strike out blindly and break something. The fury burst in his system. He drove his fists into the couch and yelled without meaning or intelligence, a wild outraged cry. Then he rolled on his side, facing the door. The fierce anger abated. He compressed his mouth into a thin shaking line.

"Mary," he whispered in lonely terror.

The door opened and Mary came in.

Wade sat up stiffly, gaping, blinking, believing himself mad.

She was still there, dressed in white, her eyes warm with love for him.

He couldn't speak. He doubted that his muscles would sustain him, yet he rose up waveringly.

She came to him.

There was no terror in her look. She was smiling with a radiant happiness. Her comforting hand brushed over his cheek.

A sob broke on his lips at the touch of her hand. He reached out with shaking arms and grasped her, embraced her tightly, pressing his face into her silky hair.

"Oh, Mary," he mumbled.

"Shhh, my darling," she whispered, "It's all right now."

Happiness flooded his veins as he kissed her warm lips. The terror and lonely fright were gone. He ran trembling fingers over her face.

They sat down on the couch. He kept caressing her arms, her hands, her face, as though he couldn't believe it was true.

"How did you get here?" he asked, in a shaky voice.

"I'm here. Isn't that enough?"

"Mary."

He pressed his face against her soft body. She stroked his hair and he was comforted.

Then, as he sat there, eyes tightly shut, a terrible thought struck him.

"Mary," he said, almost afraid to ask.

"Yes, my darling."

"How did you get here?"

"Is it so—"

"How?" He sat up and stared into her eyes. "Did they send the time-chamber for you?" he asked.

He knew they hadn't, but he clutched at the possibility.

She smiled sadly. "No, my dear," she said.

He felt himself shudder. He almost drew back in revulsion.

"Then you're—" His eyes were wide with shock, his face drained of color.

She pressed against him and kissed his mouth.

"Darling," she begged, "does it matter so? It's me. See? It's really me. Oh my darling, we have so little time. Please love me. I've waited so long for this moment."

He pressed his cheek against hers, clutching her to him.

"Oh my God, Mary, Mary," he groaned. "What am I to do? How long will you stay?"

*A person, from your period, say, would last about three quarters of an hour.* The remembrance of Clemolk's words was like a whip lash on tender flesh.

"Forty min—" he started and couldn't finish.

"Don't think about it darling," she begged. "Please. We're together for now."

But, as they kissed, a thought made his flesh crawl.

I am kissing a dead woman—his mind would not repress the words—I am holding her in my arms.

They sat quietly together. Wade's body grew more tense with each passing second.

How soon? . . . Disintegrate . . . How could he bear it? Yet he could bear less to leave her.

"Tell me about our baby," he said, trying to drive away the fear. "Was it a boy or a girl?"

She was silent.

"Mary?"

"You don't know? No, of course you don't."

"Know what?"

"I can't tell you about our child."

"Why?"

"I died when it was born."

He tried to speak but the words shattered in his throat. Finally he could ask, "Because I didn't return?"

"Yes," she replied softly. "I had no right to. But I didn't want to live without you."

"And they refuse to let me go back," he said bitterly. Then he ran his fingers through her thick hair and kissed her. He looked into her face. "Listen," he said, "I'm going to return."

"You can't change what's done."

"If I come back," he said, "it *isn't* done. I can change it."

She looked at him strangely. "Is it possible—" she began, and her words died in a groan. "No, no, it can't be!"

"Yes!" he said, "It *is* poss—" He stopped abruptly, his

heart lurching wildly. She had been speaking of something else.

Under his fingers her left arm was disappearing. The flesh seemed to be dissolving, leaving her arm rotted and shapeless.

He gasped in horror. Terrified, she looked down at her hands. They were falling apart, bits of flesh spiraling away like slender streamers of white smoke.

"No!" she cried. "Don't let it happen!"

"Mary!"

She tried to take his hands but she had none herself. Quickly she bent over and kissed him. Her lips were cold and shaking.

"So soon," she sobbed. "Oh, go away! Don't watch me, Robert! Please don't watch me!" Then she started up, crying out, "Oh, my dear, I had hoped for—"

The rest was lost in a soft, guttural bubbling. Her throat was beginning to disintegrate.

Wade leaped up and tried to embrace her to hold back the horror, but his clutch only seemed to hasten the dissolution. The sound of her breaking down became a terrible hiss.

He staggered back with a shriek, holding his hands before him as though to ward off the awful sight.

Her body was breaking apart in chunks. The chunks split into fizzing particles which dissolved in the air. Her hands and arms were gone. The shoulders started to disappear. Her feet and legs burst apart and the swirls of gaseous flesh spun up into the air.

Wade crashed into the wall, his shaking hands over his face. He didn't want to look, but he couldn't help himself. Drawing his fingers down, he watched in a sort of palsied fascination.

Now her chest and shoulders were going. Her chin and lower face were flowing into an amorphous cloud of flesh that gyrated like windblown snow.

Last to go were her eyes. Alone, hanging on a veil of gray wall, they burned into his. In his mind came the last message from her living mind: "Good-bye, my darling. I shall always love you."

He was alone.

His mouth hung open, and his eyes were circles of dumb unbelief. For long minutes he stood there, shivering helplessly, looking hopefully—hopelessly—around the room. There was nothing, not the least sensory trace of her passing.

He tried to walk to the couch, but his legs were useless blocks of wood. And all at once the floor seemed to fly up into his face.

White pain gave way to a sluggish black current that claimed his mind.

Clemolk was sitting in the chair.

"I'm sorry you took it so badly," he said.

Wade said nothing, his gaze never leaving the historian's face. Heat rose in his body, his muscles twitched.

"We could probably re-form her again," Clemolk said carelessly, "but her body would last an even shorter period the second time. Besides we haven't the—"

"What do you want?"

"I thought we might talk some more about 1975 while there's—"

"You thought that, did you!" Wade threw himself into a sitting position, eyes bright with crazed fury. "You keep me prisoner, you torture me with the ghost of my wife. Now you want to talk!"

He jolted to his feet, fingers bent into arcs of taut flesh.

Clemolk stood up, too, and reached into his robe pocket. The very casualness of the move further enraged Wade. When the historian drew out the plastic case, Wade knocked it to the floor with a snarl.

"Stop this," Clemolk said mildly, his visage still unruffled.

"I'm going back," roared Wade. "I'm going back and you're not stopping me!"

"I'm not stopping you," said Clemolk, the first signs of

peevishness sounding in his voice. "You're stopping yourself. I've told you. You should have considered what you were doing before entering your time-chamber. And, as for your Mary—"

The sound of her name pronounced with such dispassionate smugness broke the floodgates of Wade's fury. His hand shot out and fastened around Clemolk's thin ivory column of neck.

"Stop," Clemolk said, his voice cracking. "You can't go back. I tell you—"

His fish eyes were popping and blurred. A gurgle of delicate protest filled his throat as his frail hands fumbled at Wade's clutching fingers. A moment later the historian's eyes rolled back and his body went limp. Wade released his fingers and put Clemolk down on the couch.

He ran to the door, his mind filled with conflicting plans. The door wouldn't open. He pushed it, threw his weight against it, tried to dig his nails along its edge to pull it open. It was tightly shut. He stepped back, his face contorted with hopeless frenzy.

Of course!

He sprang to Clemolk's inert body, reached in the robe pocket, and drew out the small control board. It had no connections in the robe. Wade pushed a button. The great sign was above him: HISTORY IS LIVING. With an impatient gasp, Wade pushed another, still another. He heard his voice.

". . . The governmental system was based on the existence of three branches, two of which were supposedly subject to popular vote. . . ."

He pushed another button—and yet another.

The door seemed to draw a heavy breath and opened noiselessly. Wade ran to it and through it. It closed behind him.

Now to find the machine lab. What if the students were there? He had to risk it.

He raced down the padded hallway, looking for the tube door. It was a nightmare of running. Back and forth he rushed frantically, muttering to himself. He stopped and forced himself back, pushing buttons as he went, ignoring sounds and sights around him—the fading walls, the speaking dead. He almost missed the tube door as he passed it. Its outline blended with the wall.

"Stop!"

He heard the weak cry behind him and glanced hurriedly over his shoulder. Clemolk, stumbling along the hall, waving him down. He must have recovered and got out while Wade was carrying on his desperate search.

Wade entered the tube quickly, and the door slid shut. He breathed a sign of relief as he felt the chamber rush through its tunnel. Something made him turn around. He gasped at the sight of the uniformed man who sat on the bench facing him. In the man's hand was a dull black tube that pointed straight at Wade's chest.

"Sit down," said the man.

Defeated, Wade slumped down in a dejected heap. Mary. The name was a broken lament in his mind.

"Why do you re-forms get so excited?" the man asked. "Why do you? Answer me that?"

Wade looked up, a spark of hope igniting in him. The man thought—

"I—expected to go soon," Wade said hurriedly. "In a matter of minutes. I wanted to get down to the machine lab."

"Why there, for heaven's sake?"

"I heard there was a time-chamber there," Wade said anxiously. "I thought—"

"Thought you'd use it?"

"Yes, that's it. I want to go back to my own time. I'm lonely."

"Haven't you been told?" asked the man.

"Told what?"

The tube sighed to a halt. Wade started up. The man waved his weapon and Wade sank down again. Had they passed it? "As soon as your re-formed body returns to air," the man was saying, "your psychic force returns to the original moment of death—hrumph—separation from the body I mean."

Wade was distracted by nervous fear. "What?" he asked vaguely, looking around.

"Personal force, personal force," bumbled the man. "At the moment it leaves your re-formed body, it will return to the moment you originally—uh—died. In your case that would be—when?"

"I don't understand."

The man shrugged. "No matter, no matter. Take my word for it. You'll soon be back in your own time."

"What about the machine lab?" Wade asked again.

"Next stop," said the man.

"Can we go there, I mean?"

"Oh," grumbled the man, "I suppose I could drop in and take a look at it. Think they'd let me know. Never any cooperation with the military. Invariably—" His voice trailed off. "No," he resumed. "On second thought, I'm in a hurry."

Wade watched the man lower his weapon. He clenched his teeth and braced himself to lunge.

"Well," said the man, "on third thought..."

Closing his eyes, Wade slumped back and exhaled a long shuddering breath through his pale lips.

It was still intact, its gleaming metal reflecting the tiers of bright overhead lights—and the circular door was open.

There was only one student in the lab. He was sitting at a bench. He looked up as they entered.

"Can I help you, Commander?" he asked.

"No need. No need," said the officer in an annoyed voice. "The re-form and myself are here to see the time-chamber." He waved toward the platform. "That it?"

"Yes, that's it," said the student, looking at Wade. Wade averted his face. He couldn't tell whether the student was one of the four who had been there before. They all looked alike. The student went back to his work.

Wade and the Commander stepped up on the platform. The

Commander peered into the interior of the sphere.

"Well," he mused, "who brought it here, I'd like to know."

"I don't know," Wade answered. "I've never seen one."

"And you thought you could use it!" The Commander laughed.

Wade glanced around nervously to make sure the student wasn't watching. Turning back, he scanned the sphere rapidly and saw that it wasn't fastened in any way. He started as a loud buzzer sounded and looking around quickly, saw the student push a button on the wall. He tightened in fear.

On a small teleview screen built into the wall, Clemolk's face had appeared. Wade couldn't hear the historian's voice but his face showed excitement at last.

Wade spun back, facing the chamber, and asked, "Think I could see what it's like inside?"

"No, no," said the Commander. "You'll play tricks."

"I won't," he said, "I'll just—"

"Commander!" cried the student.

The Commander turned. Wade gave him a shove, and the corpulent officer staggered forward, his arms flailing the air for balance, and a look of astonished outrage on his face.

Wade dove into the time chamber, cracking his knees on the metal deck, and scrambled around.

The student rushing toward the sphere, pointing one of those dull black tubes ahead of him.

Wade grabbed the heavy door and with a grunt of effort pulled it shut. The heavy circle of metal grated into place, cutting off a flash of blue flame that was directed at him. Wade spun the wheel around feverishly until the door was securely fixed.

They would be cutting the chamber open any moment.

His eyes swept over th dials as his fingers worked on the strap buckles. He saw that the main dial was still set at five hundred years and raching over, flipped it to reverse position.

Everything seemed ready. He had to take a chance that it was. There was no time to check. Already a deadly cutting flame might be directed at the metal globe.

The straps were fastened. Wade braced himself and threw the main switch. Nothing happened. A cry of mortal terror broke through his lips. His eyes darted around. His fingers shook over the control board as he tested the connections.

A plug was loose. Grabbing it with both hands to steady it, he slid it into its socket. At once the chamber began to vibrate. The high screech of its mechanism was music to him.

The universe poured by again, the black night washing over him like ocean waves. This time he didn't lose consciousness.

He was secure.

The chamber stopped vibrating. The silence was almost deafening. Wade sat breathlessly in the semidarkness, gasping in air. Then he grabbed the wheel and turned it quickly. He kicked open the door and jumped down into the apparatus lab of Fort College and looked around, hungry for the sight of familiar things.

The lab was empty. One wall light shone down bleakly in the silence, casting great shadows of machines, sending his own shadow leaping up the walls. He touched benches, stools, gauges, machines, anything, just to convince himself that he was back.

"It's real." He said it over and over.

An overpowering weakness of relief fell over him like a mantle. He leaned against the chamber. Here and there he saw black marks on the metal, and pieces of it were hanging loose. He felt almost a love for it. Even partly destroyed it had gotten him back.

Suddenly he looked at the clock. Two in the morning. . . . Mary. . . . He had to get home. Quickly, quickly.

The door was locked. He fumbled for keys, got the door open and rushed down the hall. The building was deserted. He reached the front door, unlocked it, remembered to lock it behind him, although he was shaking with excitement.

He tried to walk, but he kept breaking into a run, and his mind raced ahead in anticipation. He was on the porch, through the doorway, rushing up to the bedroom. . . . Mary, Mary, he was calling. . . . He was bursting through the doorway. . . . She was standing by the window. She whirled, saw him, a look of glorious happiness crossed her face. She cried out in tearful joy. . . . They were holding each other, kissing; together, together.

"Mary," he murmured in a choked-up voice as, once more, he began running.

The tall black Social Sciences Building was behind him. Now the campus was behind him, and he was running happily down University Avenue.

The street lights seemed to waver before him. His chest heaved with shuddering breaths. A burning ache stabbed at his side. His mouth fell open. Exhausted, he was forced to slow down to a walk. He gasped in air, started to run again.

Only two more blocks.

Ahead the dark outline of his home stood out against the sky. There was a light in the living room. She was awake. She hadn't given up!

His heart flew out to her. The desire for her warm arms was almost more than he could bear.

He felt tired. He slowed down, felt his limbs trembling violently. Excitement. His body ached. He felt numb.

He was on their walk. The front door was open. Through the screen door, he could see the stairs to the second floor. He paused, his eyes glittering with a sick hunger.

"Home," he muttered.

He staggered up the path, up the porch steps. Shooting pains wracked his body. His head felt as though it would explode.

He pulled open the screen door and lurched to the living-room arch.

John Randall's wife was sleeping on the couch.

There was no time to talk. He wanted Mary. He turned and stumbled to the stairs. He started up.

He tripped, almost fell. He groped for the banister with his right hand. A scream gurgled up and died in his throat. *The hand was dissolving in air*. His mouth fell open as the horror struck him.

"No!" He tried to scream it but only a mocking wheeze escaped his lips.

He struggled up. The disintegration was going on faster. His hands. His wrists. They were flying apart. He felt as though he had been thrown into a vat of burning acid.

His mind twisted over itself as he tried to understand. And all the while he kept dragging himself up the stairs, now on his ankles, now on his knees, the corroded remnants of his disappearing legs.

Then he knew all of it. Why the chamber door was locked. Why they wouldn't let him see his own corpse. Why his body had lasted so long. It was because he had reached 2475 alive and *then* had died. Now he had to return to that year. He could not be with her *even in death*.

"Mary!"

He tried to scream for her. She had to know. But no sound came. He felt pieces of his throat falling out. Somehow he had to reach her, let her know that he had come back.

He reached the top of the landing and through the open door of their room saw her lying on the bed, sleeping in exhausted sorrow.

He called. No sound. Tears of rage poured from his anguished eyes. Now he was at the door, trying to force himself into the room.

*There'd be no life for me without you.*

Her remembered words tortured him. His crying was like a gentle bubbling of lava.

Now he was almost gone. The last of him poured over the rug like a morning mist, the blackness of his eyes like dark shiny beads in a swirling fog.

"Mary, Mary—" he could only think it now "—how very much I love you."

She didn't awaken.

He willed himself closer and drank in the fleeting sight of her. A massive despair weighed on his mind. A faint groan fluttered over his wraith.

Then, the woman, smiling in her uneasy sleep, was alone

in the room except for two haunted eyes which hung suspended for a moment and then were gone; like tiny worlds that flare up in birth and, in the same moment, die.

## The Jazz Machine

I had the weight that night
I mean I had the blues and no one hides the blues away
You got to wash them out
Or you end up riding a slow drag to nowhere
You got to let them fly
I mean you got to

I play trumpet in this barrelhouse off Main Street
Never mind the name of it
It's like scumpteen other cellar drink dens
Where the downtown ofays bring their loot and jive talk
And listen to us try to blow out notes
As white and pure as we can never be

Like I told you, I was gully low that night
Brassing at the great White way
Lipping back a sass in jazz that Rone got off in words
And died for
Hitting at the jug and loaded
Spiking gin and rage with shaking miseries
I had no food in me and wanted none
I broke myself to pieces in a hungry night

This white I'm getting off on showed at ten
Collared him a table near the stand
And sat there nursing at a glass of wine
Just casing us
All the way into the late watch he was there

He never budged or spoke a word
But I could see that he was picking up
On what was going down
He got into my mouth, man
He bothered me

At four I crawled down off the stand
And that was when this ofay stood and put his grabber
on my arm
"May I speak to you?" he asked
The way I felt I took no shine
To pink hands wrinkling up my gaberdine
"Broom off, stud," I let him know
"Please," he said, "I have to speak to you."

Call me blowtop, call me Uncle Tom
Man, you're not far wrong
Maybe my brain was nowhere
But I sat down with Mister Pink
and told him—lay his racket
"You've lost someone," he said.

It hit me like a belly chord
"What do you know about it, white man?"
I felt that hating pick up tempo in my guts again
"I don't know anything about it," he replied
"I only know you've lost someone
"*You've told it to me with your horn a hundred times.*"
I felt evil crawling in my belly
"Let's get this straight," I said
"Don't hype me, man; don't give me stuff"
"Listen to me then," he said

"Jazz isn't only music
"It's a language too
"A language born of protest
"Torn in bloody ragtime from the womb of anger and despair
"A secret tongue with which the legions of abused

"Cry out their misery and their troubled hates."
"This language has a million dialects and accents
"It may be a tone of bittersweetness whispered in a brass-
lined throat
"Or rush of frenzy screaming out of reed mouths
"Or hammering at strings in vibrant piano hearts
"Or pulsing, savage, under taut-drawn hides

"In dark-peaked stridencies it can reveal the aching core of
sorrow
"Or cry out the new millennium
"Its voices are without number
"Its forms beyond statistic
"It is, in very fact, *an endless tonal revolution*
"The pleading furies of the damned
"Against the cruelty of their damnation
"I know this language, friend," he said.

"What about my—?" I began and cut off quick
"Your—*what*, friend?" he inquired
"Someone near to you; I know that much
"Not a woman though; your trumpet wasn't grieving for a
woman loss
"Someone in your family; your father maybe
"Or your brother."

I gave him words that tiger-prowled behind my teeth
"You're hanging over trouble, man
"Don't break the thread
"Give it to me straight."
So Mister Pink leaned in and laid it down
"I have a sound machine," he said
"Which can convert the forms of jazz
"Into the sympathies which made them
"If, into my machine, I play a sorrowing blues
"From out the speaker comes the human sentiment
"Which felt those blues
"And fashioned them into the secret tongue of jazz."

He dug the same old question stashed behind my eyes
"How do I know you've lost someone?" he asked
"I've heard so many blues and stomps and strutting jazzes
"Changed, in my machine, to sounds of anger, hopelessness
and joy
"That I can understand the language now
"The story that you told was not a new one
"Did you think you were inviolate behind your tapestry of
woven brass?"

"Don't hype me, man," I said
I let my fingers rigor mortis on his arm
He didn't ruffle up a hair
"If you don't believe me, come and see," he said
"Listen to my machine
"Play your trumpet into it
"You'll see that everything I've said is true."
I felt shivers like a walking bass inside my skin
"Well, will you come?" he asked.

Rain was pressing drum rolls on the roof
As Mister Pink turned tires onto Main Street
I sat dummied in his coupé
My sacked-up trumpet on my lap
Listening while he rolled off words
Like Stacy runnings on a tinkle box

"Consider your top artists in the genre
"Armstrong, Bechet, Waller, Hines
"Goodman, Mezzrow, Spanier, dozens more both male and
female
"Jews and Negroes all and why?
"Why are the greatest jazz interpreters
"Those who live beneath the constant gravity of prejudice?
"I think because the scaldings of external bias
"Focus all their vehemence and suffering
"To a hot, explosive core
"And, from this nucleus of restriction

"Comes all manner of fissions, violent and slow
"Breaking loose in brief expression
"Of the tortures underneath
"Crying for deliverance in the unbreakable code of jazz."
He smiled. *"Unbreakable till now,"* he said.
"Rip bop doesn't do it
"Jump and mop-mop only cloud the issue
"They're like jellied coatings over true response
"Only the authentic jazz can break the pinions of repression
"Liberate the heart-deep mournings
"Unbind the passions, give freedom to the longing essence
"You understand?" he asked.
"I understand," I said, knowing why I came.

Inside the room, he flipped the light on, shut the door
Walked across the room and slid away a cloth that covered his
machine
"Come here," he said
I suspicioned him of hyping me but good
His jazz machine was just a jungleful of scraggy tubes and
wheels
And scumpteen wires boogity-boogity
Like a black-snake brawl
I double-o'ed the heap
"That's really in there, man," I said
And couldn't help but smile a cutting smile
Right off he grabbed a platter, stuck it down
"Heebie-Jeebies; Armstrong
"First, I'll play the record by itself," he said

Any other time I'd bust my conk on Satchmo's scatting
But I had the crawling heavies in me
And I couldn't even loosen up a grin
I stood there feeling nowhere
While Daddy-O was tromping down the English tongue
*Rip-bip-dee-doo-dee-doot-doo!*
The Satch recited in his Model T baritone
Then white man threw a switch

## SHOCK III

In one hot second all the crazy scat was nixed
Instead, all pounding in my head
There came a sound like bottle blowtops scuffling up a
jamboree
Like twenty tongue-tied hipsters in the next apartment
Having them a ball
Something frosted up my spine
I felt the shakes do get-off chorus in my gut
And even though I knew that Mister Pink was smiling at me
I couldn't look him back
My heart was set to knock a doorway through my chest
Before he cut his jazz machine

"You see?" he asked.
I couldn't talk. He had the up on me
"Electrically, I've caught the secret heart of jazz
"Oh, I could play you many records
"That would illustrate the many moods
"Which generate this complicated tongue
"But I would like for you to play in my machine
"Record a minute's worth of solo
"Then we'll play the record through the other speaker
"And we'll hear exactly what you're feeling
"Stripped of every sonic superficial. Right?"

I had to know
I couldn't leave that place no more than fly
So, while white man set his record maker up,
I unsacked my trumpet, limbering up my lip
All the time the heebies rising in my craw
Like ice cubes piling

Then I blew it out again
The weight
The dragging misery
The bringdown blues that hung inside me
Like twenty irons on a string
And the string stuck to my guts with twenty hooks

That kept on slicing me away
I played for Rone, my brother
Rone who could have died a hundred different times and
 ways
Rone who died, instead, down in the Murder Belt
Where he was born
Rone who thought he didn't have to take that same old stuff
Rone who forgot and rumbled back as if he was a man
And not a spade
Rone who died without a single word
Underneath the boots of Mississippi peckerwoods
Who hated him for thinking he was human
And kicked his brains out for it

That's what I played for
I blew it hard and right
And when I finished and it all came rushing back on me
Like screaming in a black-walled pit
I felt a coat of evil on my back
With every scream a button that held the dark coat closer
Till I couldn't get the air

That's when I crashed my horn on his machine
That's when I knocked it on the floor
And craunched it down and kicked it to a thousand pieces
"You fool!" That's what he called me
"*You damned black fool!*"
 All the time until I left

I didn't know it then
I thought that I was kicking back for every kick
That took away my only brother
But now it's done and I can get off all the words
I should have given Mister Pink

Listen, white man; listen to me good
Buddy ghee, it wasn't you
I didn't have no hate for you

## SHOCK III

Even though it was your kind that put my brother
In his final place
I'll knock it to you why I broke your jazz machine

I broke it 'cause I had to
'Cause it did just what you said it did
And, if I let it stand,
It would have robbed us of the only thing we have
That's ours alone
The thing no boot can kick away
Or rope can choke

You cruel us and you kill us
But listen, white man,
These are only needles in our skin
But if I'd let you keep on working your machine
You'd know all our secrets
And you'd steal the last of us
And we'd blow away and never be again
Take everything you want, Man
You will because you have
But don't come scuffling for our souls.

# The Disinheritors

Let me tell you about one of the last persons who went on a picnic with her husband, George Grady.

This person's name was Alice and she had blonde hair and a mind of her own. She was twenty-eight by the calendar and her husband was thirty-two. They liked to daydream sometimes as most people do. That's not why they went on a picnic but it bears mentioning.

George worked for the city. This meant working six days and having one free. The week they went on the picnic, the day was Wednesday.

So on this Wednesday morning, Alice and George got up very early, even before their electric rooster had clarioned the dawn. They whispered while they dressed and completed their toilets, and then went downstairs to the kitchen.

They had breakfast and made sandwiches and sliced pickles and George took out hard-boiled egg yolks, mixed them with pepper and other condiments and shoved the result back into the eggs again and called them works of art.

Then, when they had all the sandwiches neatly folded into waxed paper and the thermos bottle gurgling full with coffee, they tumbled out of their little homestead.

Their automobile stood waiting in the early-morning air. Into its damp, oily interior they piled and went chugging off to the country, up hills and down dales and so on. They drove until there were no more billboards, which is a long drive from any city.

When they reached the point where nature had a thin

breathing ground before dying into the next suburb, George turned off the superhighway and drove down an old lane encrusted with high grass and bushes and foliage-dripping trees.

At length he turned the nose of their faithful runabout into a rich forest glade. He shut off the motor and they got out and spread a blanket on the ground where they could look over a mirror-sheened lake.

Then they sat down and admired God's handiwork and made appropriate remarks. Alice pulled up her thin knees and put her equally thin arms around them. George took off his hat and arranged the few remaining strands of his hair. As usual he regaled Alice with tales about the boys at work and what cards they were. Alice didn't care. Neither did George, for that matter.

After a while they ate the food in the mesh basket and smacked their respective lips and said there's nothing like eating in the country. And George ate five sandwiches and belched to the north.

Then, when filled up to the chin line, he groaned an immense groan, loosened his belt and rolled on his back. He yawned and, through his gaping gold-toothed mouth, announced his intentions of sleeping the ensuing two years.

Alice said, let's take a walk and admire the scenery. She said we need it to digest all the food we ate. She said it's a crime to waste all this beauty, this is such a gorgeous, gorgeous spot. She said George are you asleep and he said yes.

She got up clucking accusingly.

She left him snoring and walked out of the glade and down a wood-rimmed path.

It was a warm day. Sunlight patted the earth with warm hands. Overhead the breeze whispered in the leaves and the rustle of the woodlands was a song. Birds chirped and twittered and gave forth, and Alice was consumed with a passion for Nature. She skipped. And she sang.

She reached a hill and walked up with a mountaineer's crouch. At the summit she pushed lean fists into her hips and looked down possessively at the dark forest floor ahead.

Down there it looked like a murky auditorium with all the trees like patient customers waiting for the show to start. Hardly any light penetrated the thick canopy of their leafy coiffures.

Alice clapped her hands in wordless delight and went down a path which seemed to have appeared out of nowhere, and had. Leaves crackled incantations beneath her descending feet.

At the foot of the path, she found a little bridge arching its moldy back over a brook that gurgled and bubbled over smooth stones.

Alice stood on the bridge and peered into the crystal torrent. She saw herself as in a melting glass. Her reflection ran, burst, and jumped together again. It made her giggle.

I am lost in the woods, she said to herself. I am li'l Goldilocks and I am lost in the nassy ole woods.

She tittered, wrinkling her thin-cheeked face.

Then she wondered what on earth had made her think of Goldilocks after all those years. She put her eyebrows together. They huddled in a conference. Brain cells tried harder.

She let it go.

That was a mistake.

I am Goldilocks, she insisted in song as she turned from the rail and skipped off the squeaking bridge.

Alice stopped short and gaped.

My God, she said.

There was a little house in the deepest shadow of the glade, sitting at the feet of the forest. That's odd, Alice said to no one. I didn't see that house before. Did the shadows hide it then? I didn't see it at all from the top of the hill.

And, of course, she hadn't.

Alice crunched over the leafy woods rug toward the little house.

Half of her tugged back, sensing a strangeness. Here she had just finished saying that she was Goldilocks. And the next second *there* was a little house and if it wasn't the house of the three bears, then what was it?

She advanced with timid, half-cowed steps. Then she stopped.

It was a cute house. Just like a fairytale house with carved eaves and sills and frames. Alice got a kick out of it. She skipped up to the house feeling young.

She decided to talk in infantile gibberish as she peered through a dusty pane.

Ooh me ooh my, she cooed, isn't this a pwitty little housey wousey.

She couldn't see the inside very clearly. The windows were blurry. I shall go to the door; the thought arranged itself from the mass of incohesions in her brain. She believd it to be her own thought and went to the door.

She touched it. She pushed it open. Wow bwidge, she said, and peered in.

It was just like the room in the illustration from her Goldilocks book, which she hadn't looked in for twenty years.

Twenty? The ghastly realization weakened her delight. She pouted over the brutality of time.

Then she said, I won't even think about *that*. I'll be gay.

So, little Goldilocks went into the little house and there in the middle of the room were three chairs.

Well, I'll be goddamned, said Alice, not preserving the spirit of the moment very well.

She looked at the chair incredulously.

There was a big one. There was a mama-size one. There was the baby one.

Ulp, said Alice.

She looked around. Everything fit. She was astounded. No kidding. This was it. Insane. But as true as she was standing there.

Alice went over to the big chair. She wondered what this all added up to. Of course, she couldn't guess.

Her lips toyed with the idea of smiling as she perched herself gingerly on the edge of the papa chair. A tentative giggle erased gravity from her plain features. She felt young again. I'm li'l Goldilocks and I'll kill the first love-child that says I ain't.

She looked around with lips fumbling to repress a smile of wicked delight. I don't like this chair, she thought. I don't like it because I'm Goldilocks and I'm not supposed to like it.

She sat bolt upright.

I really *am* Goldilocks, she thought. I'm living it out fair and square.

This was a giddy thought for Mrs. Alice Grady, wed a decade, childless, with graying strands of hair and a dream-world that life had stepped on.

I don't like this chair, she declared.

And, oddly enough, she didn't like it. So she stood up. The momentary thought struck her that George would have got a charge out of this little place. Well, it was his own fault, sleeping away his life. She couldn't be blamed for thinking that.

Alice grew up for a moment in wondering who owned this charming little house. Was it an exhibit for some fur-coat company, some chair manufacturer? Eh? she said, but the walls answered not.

She went to the window and peered out.

She couldn't see very well. But she did notice that it was getting darker.

However, there were still poles of sunlight leaning against the treetops and shafting into the earth. Alice stared at the golden ribbons and angling through the gloom. She sighed. It was a fairy tale, no fooling. It was unreality becoming real.

This frightened her.

Because people don't care for unreality becoming real. It pricks their well-fed minds, you see, with something like a hunger pang. They prefer the logical stuffiness of expectancy. It is only at certain times that they weaken, letting imagination in.

That's the time to get them.

So, frightened by shapeless apprehension, Alice clacked heels to the door. It opened without trouble. And that made the difference.

She said, oh, what the hell, why be a worry wart? Once a month maybe, with luck, George takes me out and this is the day for this month so I'm not going to waste it.

She turned and went back into the room with an air of satisfied bravado.

She tried the second chair just for the sake of plot. Uh-uh, she said in piping girlish tones. She stood up with churling disdain on her face.

Sidestepping, she plopped herself down on the smallest chair. Ah, *ha*, she declared assertively, this chair is the schmaltz. I will sit here and think.

She thought.

Now this *is* odd. Where did this house come from? Does it belong to some eccentric millionaire? No, not in a government park. Then what did it mean? Who lived there? Tell me three bears do, she said to herself, and I'll give you a shot in the teeth.

But if it wasn't three bears, who was it? She scratched her head. Or were it? Or...

Giving it up, Alice jumped up and ran into the next room.

Well, I'll be double-damned, she proclaimed in astonishment.

There was a table.

Just like the table in her childhood book, *The Three Bears*. A low, rough-hewn table, stained and aged.

And right on this table were three steaming bowls of porridge.

Alice's jaw sagged. This was a kick in the pants and no joke. What was there to make of it?

She stared at the table and the bowls, and a shiver ran down her twenty-eight-plus-year-old spine. She glanced fearfully over her shoulder. Don't know as I care to run into three bears, she said in awed tones.

Her brow pushed together into fleshy rills and ridges. This is too much, she thought. To think of living a fairy tale is one thing. To live it is another thing. This is just a little bit bone-chilling. I know there's a logical explanation for all this but...

This is their highest and lowest moment. They always know there's a logical explanation. But their boundaries of logic are always too narrow to include the explanation that does exist.

So Alice sought for solidity.

I just left George, she said. He was snoring on the ground full of logical deviled eggs and natural pickles and tangible coffee. And we are married according to solid tradition and we live at a substantial 184 Sumpter Street. George makes a corporeal $192.80 per week and we play bridge with the flesh and blood Nelsons.

She was still frightened.

Locating a lump in her throat, she swallowed it. She said, I think I'll be going now.

But she didn't move. She said, come on feet; move. But the feet remained idle. She was losing control. Now I am scared she said, scared motionless. Or maybe I'm not as frightened as I think I am. After all, she told herself, this is only a weird coincidence. This is probably the house of three nutty old people who, when they see someone coming, put three different-sized bowls of porridge on the table and hide in a closet.

Hello! called Goldilocks, is anyone t'home?

Not a soul answered and the wind chuckled evilly down the chimney.

Hello? called Alice, wishing that a crotchety old man would rush in and say—ho! what are you doing in this government museum, you interloper, it's past closing time; out you go!

No answer. No sound. Just a dead quiet house and three porridge bowls breathing aromatic steam into the air.

Alice sniffed.

Mighty good, she had to admit. But she said, I'll be switched if I eat any because, well, for one reason, I just ate a whole pile of food and I'm not at all. . .*Good God!*

Alice was starving.

Or she believed she was. Same thing. It was getting to her.

Alice got scared for real, and crossed her arms which had gone goose-fleshed. She backed away into the next room. She bumped into the papa chair and cried out—oh!

She stood shivering for a moment.

Then she calmed down. After all, she reasoned, was anyone hooting at her. Had she seen any ghostly faces? Had any invisible fingers clawed at her? No!

And that's the way they figure, of course. If they don't see things that fit into the pattern of what they think of as frightening and evil, they don't worry about anything. A strength. And a weakness.

So Alice was calm again. Were there three bears within twenty miles? In the zoo. Behind thick bars. What was the worry?

It was a little house that belonged to someone. That was all. A papa and a mama and a baby. Or three old ladies of diminishing stature. Or three retired men. They lived there and, at the moment, they were out chopping wood or getting water or gathering nuts in May.

It was all right. Quite all right. Soon she would leave and run back up the hill to George and tell him what he'd missed. And next Thursday, at bridge with the flesh and blood Nelsons, would she have an anecdote or would she have an anecdote?

Alice went back into the other room again. She muttered to her little self, I'll be a cwoss-eyed, knock-kneed, pigeon-toed, lop-eared I don't know what. Here I must have ate at least a gross of basket lunch. And now I'm hungry. Must have been the walk.

She sat at the table in the little chair. It occurred to her that if she fitted the little chair, the person who sat in the big chair must be about seven feet tall.

Now, do I dare, she thought. Does I have the temerity to eat some of this powwidge?

Her eyes narrowed suspiciously. Could it be that the porridge was poisoned, drugged, an oatmeal mickey?

She sniffed.

Why should it be? her mind inquired. Who in the hell is

going to leave poisoned porridge in a government park? That would constitute a felony and a misdemeanor and be damn nasty in the bargain.

She showed her teeth in a smile.

After all, she argued, it isn't every day that a gal gets a chance to play Goldilocks. Let's take advantage.

She took another giant whiff of the porridge in the big bowl. Mmmmm, she said, this smells scrumptious. She reached for the big spoon.

No, that wasn't cricket.

She reached in her dress pocket and plucked out a wooden spoon which had been a spear for the gherkins. She sniffed it. Not too pickley. Not by any means.

She took a little porridge from the edge of the big bowl, feeling like a perfect criminal when the cereal all mushed together again, forming a smooth, unbroken surface.

She inhaled the warm mealy odor, her nose wrinkling with pleasure. Oh, this is so good and warm and I'll just taste a little now and. . .*Yow!*

It was burning hot. The spoon jerked in her fingers and the porridge splattered on the floor. She looked around in frightened guilt, sucking in mouthfuls of air. Her mouth cooled, her scorched tongue became a cooling lump of numb flesh.

Damn, she muttered, why didn't I forget the plot and try the little bowl first crack out of the bag? No use running this thing into the ground. Alice still felt chipper. It is the one admirable quality these people have; a sense of humor which bubbles up to the very moment of destruction.

So Alice Grady alias Goldilocks tasted some porridge from the smallest bowl.

Ah, she said, this is just right. Haven't had anything so good since I was a kid.

And she ate it all up without a qualm.

Not only without a qualm but with a sort of perverse pleasure, wondering who was going to cry at the sight of the empty bowl.

However, when she had finished, Alice looked up from the bowl and felt guilt break out into drops on her forehead.

Now I've done it, she thought. Where do I get such nerve? This is a stranger's home. I'm no better than a housebreaker. I could be sent to jail for this. This eating I just did constitutes a burglary. I better get out and quick too, before the people come back.

She got up, and with a sense of penitence, picked up the cereal from the floor and threw it and the spoon into the cold fireplace.

She looked around and shook her head. No use trying to think otherwise. There was something definitely Fishy here.

Well I'm going now, she said loudly as though someone were arguing the point with her. I'm going back to George and tell him all about this.

First you must see if there are really three beds upstairs, said a voice in her mind that didn't sound familiar.

She frowned. Oh no, she said, I'm leaving right off.

Oh, no, said the voice insolently, you've got to see if there are three beds upstairs. You're Goldilocks, remember?

Alice looked worried. She chewed her lip. But she went to the staircase and started up. It seemed very much as if someone were piling stones in her stomach. She felt them getting heavier and heavier. They were cold stones.

She stopped abruptly and yawned.

I'm getting sleepy, she said.

That brought her up short, drove a bolt of icy dread through her. Someone with chilled hands was knocking on the door to her heart. I'm scared, she admitted at last. I want to go. I want to leave. This is spooky. It's wrong. I'm scared and I want to go.

How about getting up there and seeing if there are really three beds!

There was no use denying it. It wasn't her own mind speaking.

The porridge!

Clever girl. Too late. Too late.

She struggled to turn and go down the stairs. But she couldn't. She simply had to go to the bedroom. It wasn't a vague compulsion, it was an order. Alice Grady was losing touch. She was drifting away. With her remaining strength she tried to scream. Her throat closed up.

It was getting darker still. The hallway was dim. And her brain was whirling and her limbs felt like running lead. God protect me, she tried to whisper but the words died in a trembling of her lips. George, the name came forth in a crusty mumble. George save me!

Alice stumbled into the little bedroom, bleary-eyed, and the fear in her a jumble of words that weren't words. Tears ran down her numbed cheeks and her stomach hurt with a cutting pain. She cried out once.

Then, driven on, she went to the big bed and fell on it.

No no! cracked the voice in her head, this is too hard.

And she struggled up like an unoiled robot and fell on the second bed. Her mind called out—no, this one is too soft and you don't like it one bit!

With eyes closed and a burning fever in her body Alice staggered to her feet and then pitched across the small bed with a choking shriek.

She felt the soft coverlet pressing against her cheek. And the voice droned off into swirling blackness—this is the right bed. This is the right bed at last.

And when she woke up, she knew what it was all about.

The house was gone and she was lying on the forest leaves.

She got up with a smile and walked slowly up the night-shrouded hill. She even laughed aloud at that fool, Alice Grady, who had let stupid imagination get the better of her.

I was waiting for her in the car. She smiled a little as she slid in beside me.

"So," she said, "how long have you been one?"

"Years now," I said. "Remember that time Alice and George went to the seashore? About five years ago?"

She nodded. "Yes."

"Well, George and I went down to Davey Jones's locker with a mermaid," I told her, "and he lost his mind and I came back using his body for my home."

She smiled and I started the car.

"What about the Nelsons?" she asked.

''They've been with us for a long time,'' I said.

''How many real people are left on earth now?'' she asked.

''About fifty or so,'' I said.

''It's really very clever,'' she said. ''Alice Grady never suspected it for a second.''

''Of course not,'' I said. ''That's the charm of it.''

And it is charming how *we* are inheriting the earth. Without a shot. With no one's ever knowing.

One by one we've taken your bodies and made them our own. We've let your minds destroy themselves by letting your childishness extend itself beyond intelligence; until it reaches that inevitable point where we can gain complete control.

And soon there will be only us and no more earth people. Oh, the outward picture will remain. But the plan will change.

And until our work is done, the remainder of genuine earth people will never know about it.

A little more than fifty left.

Watch out.

You're one of them. *And you know.*

# Slaughter House

*I submit for your consideration, the following manuscript which was mailed to this office some weeks ago. It is presented with neither evidence nor judgment as to its validity. This determination is for the reader to make.*

Samuel D. Machildon, *Associate Secretary, Rand Society for Psychical Research.*

## I

This occurred many years ago. My brother Saul and I had taken a fancy to the old, tenantless Slaughter House. Since we were boys the yellow-edged pronouncement—*For Sale*—had hung lopsided in the grimy front window. We had vowed with boyish ambition that, when we were old enough, the sign must come down.

When we had attained our manhood, this aspiration somehow remained. We had a taste for the Victorian, Saul and I. His painting was akin to that roseate and buxom transcription of nature so endeared by the nineteenth-century artists. And my writing, though far from satisfactory realization, bore the definite stamp of prolixity, was marked by that meticulous sweep of ornate phrase which the modernists decry as dullness and artifice.

Thus, for the headquarters of our artistic labors, what better retreat than the Slaughter House, that structure which matched in cornice and frieze our intimate partialities? None, we decided, and acted readily on that decision.

The yearly endowment arranged by our deceased parents, albeit meager, we knew to suffice, since the house was in gross need of repair and, moreover, without electricity.

There was also, if hardly credited by us, a rumor of ghosts. Neighborhood children quite excelled each other in relating the harrowing experiences they had undergone with various of the more eminent specters. We smiled at their clever fancies, never once losing the conviction that purchase of the house would be wholly practical and satisfactory.

The real estate office bumbled with financial delight the day we took off their hands what they had long considered a lost cause, having even gone so far as to remove the house from their listings. Convenient arrangements were readily fashioned and, in a matter of hours, we had moved all belongings from our uncommodious flat to our new, relatively large house.

Several days were then spent in the most necessary task of cleaning. This presented itself as far more difficult a project than first anticipated. Dust lay heavy throughout the halls and rooms. Our energetic dusting would send clouds of it billowing expansively, filling the air with powdery ghosts of dirt. We noted in respect to that observation that many a spectral vision might thus be made explicable if the proper time were utilized in experiment.

In addition to dust on all places of lodgment, there was thick grime on glass surfaces ranging from downstairs windows to silver-scratched mirrors in the upstairs bath. There were loose banisters to repair, door locks to recondition, yards of thick rugging out of whose mat to beat decades of dust, and a multitude of other chores large and small to be performed before the house could be deemed livable.

Yet, even with grime and age admitted, that we had come

by an obvious bargain was beyond dispute. The house was completely furnished, moreover furnished in the delightful mode of the early 1900's. Saul and I were thoroughly enchanted. Dusted, aired, scrubbed from top to bottom, the house proved indeed a fascinating purchase. The dark luxurious drapes, the patterned rugs, the graceful furniture, the yellow-keyed spinet; everything was complete to the last detail, that detail being the portrait of a rather lovely young woman which hung above the living-room mantel.

When first we came upon it, Saul and I stood speechless before its artistic quality. Saul then spoke of the painter's technique and finally, in rapt adulation, discussed with me the various possibilities as to the identity of the model.

It was our final conjecture that she was the daughter or wife of the former tenant, whoever he had been, beyond having the name of Slaughter.

Several weeks passed by. Initial delight was slaked by full-time occupancy and intense creative effort.

We rose at nine, had our breakfast in the dining room, then proceeded to our work, I in my sleeping chamber, Saul in the solarium, which we had been able to improvise into a small studio. Each in our places, the morning passed quietly and effectively. We lunched at one, a small but nourishing meal and then resumed work for the afternoon.

We discontinued our labors about four to have tea and quiet conversation in our elegant front room. By this hour it was too late to go on with our work, since darkness would be commencing its surrounding pall on the city. We had chosen not to install electricity both for reasons of monetary prudence and the less sordid one of pure aesthetics.

We would not, for the world, have distorted the gentle charm of the house by the addition of blatant, sterile electric light. Indeed we preferred the flickering silence of candlelight in which to play our nightly game of chess. We needed no usurping of our silence by noxious radio bleatings, we ate our bakery bread unsinged and found our wine quite adequately cooled from the old icebox. Saul enjoyed the sense of living in the past and so did I. We asked no more.

But then began the little things, the intangible things, the things without reason.

Walking on the stairs, in the hallway, through the rooms, Saul or I, singly or together, would stop and receive the strangest impulse in our minds; of fleeting moment yet quite definite while existent.

It is difficult to express the feeling with adequate clarity. It was as if we heard something although there was no sound, as though we saw something when there was nothing before the eye. A sense of shifting presence, delicate and tenuous, hidden from all physical senses and yet, somehow, perceived.

There was no explaining it. In point of fact we never spoke of it together. It was too nebulous a feeling to discuss, incapable of being materialized into words. Restless though it made us, there was no mutual comparison of sensation nor could there be. Even the most abstract of thought formation could not approach what we were experiencing.

Sometimes I would come upon Saul casting a hurried glance over his shoulder, or surreptitiously reaching out to stroke empty air as though he expected his fingers to touch some invisible entity. Sometimes he would catch me doing the same. On occasion we would smile awkwardly, both of us appreciating the moment without words.

But our smiles soon faded. I almost think we were afraid to deride this unknown aegis for fear that it might prove itself actual. Not that my brother or I were superstitious in the least degree. The very fact that we purchased the house without paying the slightest feasance to the old wives' tales about its supposed anathema seems to belie the suggestion that we were, in any manner, inclined toward mystic apprehensions. Yet the house did seem, beyond question, to possess some strange potency.

Often, late at night, I would lie awake, knowing somehow that Saul was also awake in his room and that we both were listening and waiting, consciously certain about our expectation of some unknown arrival which was soon to be effected.

And effected it was.

## II

It was perhaps a month and a half after we had moved into Slaughter House that the first hint was shown as to the house's occupants other than ourselves.

I was in the narrow kitchen cooking supper on the small gas stove. Saul was in the dining alcove arranging the table for supper. He had spread a white cloth over the dark, glossy mahogany and, on it, placed two plates with attendant silver. A candelabrum of six candles glowed in the center of the table casting shadows over the snowy cloth.

Saul was about to place the cups and saucers beside the plates as I turned back to the stove. I twisted the knob a trifle to lower the flame under the chops. Then, as I began to open the icebox to get the wine, I heard Saul gasp loudly and, something thumped on the dining-room rug. I whirled and hurried out of the kitchen as fast as I could.

One of the cups had fallen to the floor, its handle snapping off. I hurriedly picked it up, my eyes on Saul.

He was standing with his back to the living-room archway, his right hand pressed to his cheek, a look of speechless shock contorting his handsome features.

"What is it?" I asked, placing the cup on the table.

He looked at me without answering and I noticed how his slender fingers trembled on his whitening cheek.

"Saul, what *is* it?"

"A hand," he said. "A hand. *It touched my cheek.*"

I believe my mouth fell open in surprise. I had, deep within the inner passages of my mind, been expecting something like this to happen. So had Saul. Yet now that it had, a natural sense of oppressive impact was on both of our shoulders.

We stood there in silence. How can I express my feeling at that moment? It was as though something tangible, a tide of choking air, crept over us like some shapeless, lethargic serpent. I noticed how Saul's chest moved in convulsive leaps and depressions and my own mouth hung open as I gasped for breath.

Then, in an added moment, the breathless vacuum was gone, the mindless dread dissolved. I managed to speak, trusting to break this awesome spell with words.

"Are you sure?" I asked.

His slender throat contracted. He forced a smile to his lips, a smile more frightened than pleasant.

"I hope not," he replied.

He reinforced his smile with some effort.

"Can it really be?" he went on, his joviality failing noticeably, "Can it really be that we've been duped into buying ourselves a haunted house?"

I maintained an effort to join in with his spirit of artificial gusto for the sake of our own minds. But it could not long last nor did I feel any abiding comfort in Saul's feigned composure. We were both exceptionaly hypersensitive, had been ever since our births, mine some twenty-seven years before, his twenty-five. We both felt this bodiless premonition deep in our senses.

We spoke no more of it, whether from distaste or foreboding I cannot say. Following our unenjoyable meal, we spent the remainder of the evening at pitifully conducted card games. I suggested, in one unguarded moment of fear, that it might be worth our consideration to have electrical outlets installed in the house.

Saul scoffed at my apparent submission and seemed a little more content to retain the relative dimness of candlelight than the occurrence before dinner would have seemed to make possible in him. Notwithstanding that, I made no issue of it.

We retired to our rooms quite early as we usually do. Before we separated, however, Saul said something quite odd to my way of thinking. He was standing at the head of the stairs looking down, I was about to open the door to my room.

"Doesn't it all seem familiar?" he asked.

I turned to face him, hardly knowing what he was talking about.

"Familiar?" I asked of him.

"I mean," he tried to clarify, "as though we'd been here before. No, more than just been here. Actually *lived* here."

I looked at him with a disturbing sense of alarm gnawing at my mind. He lowered his eyes with a nervous smile as though he'd said something he was just realizing he should not have said. He stepped off quickly for his room, muttering a most uncordial good night to me.

I then retired to my own room, wondering about the unusual restlessness which had seemed to possess Saul throughout the evening manifesting itself not only in his words but in his impatient card play, his fidgety pose on the chair upon which he sat, the agitated flexing of his fingers, the roving of his beautiful dark eyes about the living room. As though he were looking for something.

In my room, I disrobed, effected my toilet and was soon in bed. I had lain there about an hour when I felt the house shake momentarily and the air seemed abruptly permeated with a weird, discordant humming that made my brain throb.

I pressed my hands over my ears and then seemed to wake up, my ears still covered. The house was still. I was not at all sure that it had not been a dream. It might have been a heavy truck passing the house, thus setting the dream into motion in my upset mind. I had no way of being absolutely certain.

I sat up and listened. For long minutes I sat stock still on my bed and tried to hear if there were any sounds in the house. A burglar perhaps or Saul prowling about in quest of a midnight snack. But there was nothing. Once, while I glanced at the window, I thought I saw, out of the corner of my eye, a momentary glare of bluish light shining underneath my door. But, when I quickly turned my head, my eyes saw only the deepest of blackness and, at length, I sank back on my pillow and fell into a fitful sleep.

## III

The next day was Sunday. Frequent wakings during the night and light, troubled sleep had exhausted me. I remained in bed until ten-thirty although it was my general habit to rise promptly at nine each day, a habit I had acquired when quite young.

I dressed hastily and walked across the hall, but Saul was already up. I felt a slight vexation that he had not come in to speak to me as he sometimes did nor even looked in to tell me it was past rising time.

I found him in the living room eating breakfast from a small table he had placed in front of the mantelpiece. He was sitting in a chair that faced the portrait.

His head moved around quickly as I came in. He appeared nervous to me.

"Good morning," he said.

"Why didn't you wake me up?" I said. "You know I never sleep this late."

"I thought you were tired," he said. "What difference does it make?"

I sat down across from him, feeling rather peevish as I took a warm biscuit from beneath the napkin and broke it open.

"Did you notice the house shaking last night?" I asked.

"No. Did it?"

I made no reply to the flippant air of his counter-question. I took a bite from my biscuit and put it down.

"Coffee?" he said. I nodded curtly and he poured me a cup, apparently oblivious to my pique.

I looked around the table.

"Where is the sugar?" I asked.

"I never use it," he answered. "You know that."

"*I* use it," I said.

"Well, you weren't up, John," he replied with an antiseptic smile.

I rose abruptly and went into the kitchen. I opened up one

side of the cabinet and retrieved the sugar bowl with irritable fingers.

Then, as I passed it, about to leave the room, I tried to open the other side of the cabinet. It would not open. The door had been stuck quite fast since we moved in. Saul and I had decided in facetious keeping with neighborhood tradition that the cabinet contained shelf upon shelf of dehydrated ghosts.

At the moment, however, I was in little humor for droll fancies. I pulled at the door knob with rising anger. That I should suddenly insist on that moment to open the cabinet only reflected the ill-temper Saul's neglect could so easily create in me. I put down the sugar bowl and placed both hands on the knob.

"What on earth are you doing?" I heard Saul ask from the front room

I made no answer to his question but pulled harder on the cabinet knob. But it was as if the door were imbedded solidly into the frame and I could not loosen it the least fraction of an inch.

"What were you doing?" Saul asked as I sat down.

"Nothing," I said and the matter ended. I sat eating with little if any appetite. I do not know whether I felt more anger than hurt. Perhaps it was more a sense of injury since Saul is usually keenly sensitive to my responses, but that day he seemed not the slightest particle receptive. And it was that blasé dispassion in him, so different from his usual disposition, that had so thoroughly upset me.

Once, during the meal, I glanced up at him to discover that his eyes were directed over my shoulder, focusing on something behind me. It caused a distinct chill to excite itself across my back.

"What are you looking at?" I asked of him.

His eyes refocused themselves on me and the slight smile he held was erased from his lips.

"Nothing," he replied.

Nonetheless I twisted about in my chair to look. But there was only the portrait over the mantel and nothing more.

"The portrait?" I asked.

He made no answer but stirred his coffee with deceptive composure.

I said, "Saul, I'm talking to you."

His dark eyes on me were mockingly cold. As though they meant to say, Well, so you are but that is hardly a concern of mine, is it?

When he would not speak I chose to attempt an alleviation of this inexplicable tension which had risen between us. I put down my cup.

"Did you sleep well?" I asked.

His gaze moved up to me quickly, almost, I could not avoid the realization, almost suspiciously.

"Why do you ask?" he spoke distrustingly.

"Is it such an odd question?"

Again he made no reply. Instead he patted his thin lips with his napkin and pushed back his chair as though to leave.

"Excuse me," he muttered, more from habit than politeness, I sensed.

"Why are you being so mysterious?" I asked with genuine concern.

He was on his feet, ready to move away, his face virtually blank.

"I'm not," he said. "You're imagining things."

I simply could not understand this sudden alteration in him nor relate it to any equivalent cause. I stared incredulously at him as he turned away and began walking toward the hallway with short, impatient steps.

He turned left to pass through the archway and I heard his quick feet jumping up the carpeted steps. I sat there unable to move, looking at the spot from which he had just disappeared.

It was only after a long while that I turned once more to examine the portrait more carefully.

There seemed nothing unusual about it. My eyes moved over the well-formed shoulders to the slender, white throat, the chin, the cupid-bowed red lips, the delicately upturned nose, the frank green eyes. I had to shake my head. It was only the portrait of a woman and no more. How could this affect any man of sense? How could it affect Saul?

I could not finish my coffee but let it stand cold on the table. I rose, pushed back my chair and started upstairs. I went directly to my brother's room and turned the knob to enter, then felt a stiffening in my body as I realized he had locked himself in. I turned away from his door, tight-lipped and thoroughly annoyed, disturbed beyond control.

As I sat in my room most of the day, sporadically reading, I listened for his footsteps in the hall. I tried to reason out the situation in my mind, to resolve this alien transformation in his attitude towards me.

But there seemed no resolution save that of assuming headache, imperfect sleep or other equally dissatisfying explanations. They served not at all to decipher his uneasiness, the foreign way in which his eye regarded me, his marked disinclination to speak civilly.

It was then, against my will I must state clearly, that I began to suspect other than ordinary causes and to yield a momentary credence to local accounts of the house in which we lived. We had not spoken of that hand he had felt, but was it because we believed it was imagination or because we knew it wasn't?

Once during the afternoon, I stood in the hallway with closed eyes, listening intently as though I meant to capture some particular sound and ferret it out. In the deep quiet I stood wavering back and forth on the floor, the very stillness ringing in my ears.

I heard nothing. And the day passed with slow, lonely hours. Saul and I had a morose supper together during which he rejected all extended conversation and multiple offers of card games and chess during the later evening.

After he had finished his meal, he returned immediately to his room and I, after washing the dishes, returned to mine and soon retired.

The dream returned again, yet not in certainty a dream, I thought lying there in the early morning. And had it not been a dream only a hundred trucks could have made such a vibration as that which shook the house in my fancy. And the light which shone beneath the door was too bright for candlelight, a glaring blue lucency of illumination. And the footsteps I heard were very audible. Were they only in my dream however? I could not be sure.

## IV

It was nearly nine-thirty before I rose and dressed, strongly irritated that my work schedule was being thus altered by concern. I completed my toilet quickly and went out into the hall, anxious to lose myself in occupation.

Then, as I looked automatically toward Saul's room I noticed that the door was slightly ajar. I immediately assumed he was already up and at work above in the solarium, so I did not stop to see. Instead, I hurried downstairs to make myself a hasty breakfast, noticing as I entered the kitchen that the room was just as I had left it the night before.

After a moderate breakfast I went upstairs again and entered Saul's room.

It was with some consternation that I found him still on his bed. I say "on" rather than "in" since the blankets and sheets had been, and violently so, it appeared, thrown aside and were hanging down in twisted swirls upon the wooden floor.

Saul lay on the bottom sheet, clad only in a pajama trousers, his chest, shoulders and face dewed with tiny drops of perspiration.

I bent over and shook him once, but he only mumbled in sleep-ridden lethargy. I shook him again with hardened fingers and he rolled over angrily.

"Leave me alone," he spoke in thickened irritability. "You know I've been..."

He stopped, as though, once more, he was about to speak

of something he should not.

"You've been what?" I inquired, feeling a rising heat of aggravation in my system.

He said nothing but lay there on his stomach, his face buried in the white pillow.

I reached down and shook him again by the shoulder, this time more violently. At this he pushed up abruptly and almost screamed at me.

"Get out of here!"

"Are you going to paint?" I asked shaking nervously.

He rolled on his side and squirmed a little, preparatory to sleeping again. I turned away with a harsh breath of anger.

"You make your own breakfast," I said, feeling yet more fury at the senseless import of my words. As I pulled shut the door in leaving I thought I heard Saul laughing.

I went back to my room and started to work on my play though hardly with success. My brain could not grasp concentration. All I could think of was the uncommon way in which my pleasant life had been usurped.

Saul and I had always been exceptionally close to one another. Our lives had always been inseparable, our plans were always mutual plans, our affections invariably directed primarily upon each other. This had been so since our boyhood when in grade school other children laughingly called us The Twins in contraction of our fuller title—The Siamese Twins. And, even though I had been two years ahead of Saul in school we were always together, choosing our friends with a regard to each other's tastes and distastes, living, in short, with and for each other.

Now this; this enraging schism in our relationship. This harsh severance of comradely association, this abrupt, painful transmutation from intimacy to callous inattention.

The change was of such a gravity to me that almost immediately I began to look for the most grave of causes. And, although the implied solution seemed at the very least tenuous, I could not help but entertain it willingly. And, once more entertained, I could not remove myself from the notion.

In the quiet of my room, I pondered of ghosts.

Was it then possible that the house was haunted? Hastily I mulled over the various implications, the various intimations that the theory was verifiable.

Excluding the possibility that they were dream content, there were the heaving vibrations and the weird, high-pitched humming which had assailed my brain. There was the eerie blue light I had dreamed or actually seen beneath my door. And, finally, the most damning of evidence, there was Saul's statement that he had felt a hand on his cheek. *A cold, damp hand!*

Yet, despite all, it is a difficult thing to admit the existence of ghosts in a coldly factual world. One's very instincts rebel at the admission of such maddening possiblilty. For, once the initial step is made into the supernatural, there is no turning back, no knowing where the strange road leads except that it is quite unknown and quite terrible.

So actual were the premonitions I began to feel that I put aside my unused writing tablet and pen and rushed into the hall and to Saul's room as though something were awry there.

The ludicrous, unexpected sound of his snoring set me momentarily at ease. But my smile was short-lived, vanishing instantly when I saw the half-empty liquor bottle on his bedside table.

The shock of it made my flesh grow cold. And the thought came—he is corrupted, although I had no knowledge of its source.

As I stood there above his spread-eagled form, he groaned once and turned on his back. He had dressed, but his slept-in attire was now dishevelled and crumpled. His face, I noted, was unshaven and extremely haggard and the bloodshot gaze he directed at me was that of one stranger to another.

"What do you want?" he asked in hoarse, unnatural tones.

"Are you out of your mind?" I said. "What in God's name . . . ?"

"Get out of here," he said again to me, his brother.

I stared at his face and, although I knew it could be only the result of drink distorting his unshaven features, I could not dispel the apprehension that he was, somehow, coarse, and a shudder of strange revulsion ran through me.

I was about to take the bottle away from him when he swung at me, a wildly inaccurate flinging of the arm, his sense of direction blunted by a drink-thickened brain.

"I said, get *out* of here!" he shouted in a fury, streaks of mottled red leaping into his cheeks.

I backed away, almost in fright, then turned on my heel and hurried into the hall, trembling with the shock of my brother's unnatural behavior. I stood outside his door for a long time, listening to him toss restlessly on his bed, groaning. And I felt close to tears.

Then, without thought, I descended the darkening stairway, moved across the living room and dining alcove and entered the small kitchen. There, in the black silence, I held aloft a spluttering match and then lit the heavy candle I retrieved from the stove.

My footsteps, as I moved about the kitchen, seemed oddly muffled, as though I were hearing them through thick, cotton padding in my ears. And I began to get the most incongruous sensation that the very silence was drumming roughly in my ears.

As I passed the left hand side of the cabinet I found myself swaying heavily as though the dead, motionless air had suddenly become mobile and were buffeting me about. The silence was a roaring now and, suddenly, I clutched out for support and my twitching fingers knocked a dish onto the tile floor.

A positive shudder ran through me then because the sound of the breaking dish had been hollow and unreal, the sound of something greatly distant. If I had not seen the porcelain fragments lying on the dark tile I might have sworn the dish had not shattered at all.

With a sense of mounting restlessness I pushed my index fingers into my ears and twisted them around as if to ease what seemed an obstruction. Then I clenched my fist and struck the fastened cabinet door, almost desperate for the comfort of logical sound. But no matter how strong my blows, the sound came to my ears no louder than that of someone far away knocking at some door.

I turned hastily to the small icebox, very anxious now to make my sandwiches and coffee and be out of there, up in my room once more.

I put the bread on a tray, poured a cupful of the steaming black coffee and put the coffee pot down on its burner again. Then, with distinct trepidation, I bent over and blew out the candle.

The dining alcove and living room were oppressively dark now. My heart began to thud heavily as I moved across the rug, my footsteps muffled as I walked. I held the tray in stiff, unfeeling fingers, my gaze directed straight ahead. As I moved, my breath grew more harsh, bursting from my nostrils as I held my lips pressed tightly together lest they begin shaking with fright.

The blackness and the dead, utter silence seemed to crush in on me like solid walls. I held my throat stiff, my every muscle suspended by will for fear that relaxation would cause me to shake without control.

Halfway to the hall I heard it.

A soft, bubbling laughter which seemed to permeate the room like a cloud of sound.

A swamping wave of coldness covered my body and my footsteps halted abruptly as my legs and body stiffened.

The laughter did not cease. It continued, moving about me as if someone—or some *thing*—circled me on soundless tread, its eyes always on me. I began to tremble and, in the stillness, I could hear the rattling of the cup on my tray.

Then, suddenly, a damp, cold hand pressed against my cheek!

With a terrified howl of fear I dropped the tray and ran wildly into the hall and up the stairs, my weakening legs propelling me forward in the blackness. As I ran there was another gush of liquid laughter behind me, like a thin trail of icy air in the stillness.

I locked the door to my room and hurled my self on the bed, pulling the bedspread over myself with shaking fingers. My eyes tightly shut, I lay there with heart pounding against the mattress. And, in my mind, the hideous cognition that all my fears were justified was a knife stabbing at delicate tissues.

It was all true.

As actually as if a living human hand had touched me, I had felt that cold and soggy hand on my cheek. But what living person was down there in the darkness?

For a short time I belied to tell myself it had been Saul executing a cruel and vicious joke. But I knew it had not been, for I would have heard his footsteps and I had heard none, either before or now.

The clock was chiming ten when I was at last able to summon the courage to throw off the spread, scrabble for the box of matches on my bedside table and light the candle.

At first the guttering light assuaged fear slightly. But then I saw how little it illuminated the silent darkness and I avoided, with a shudder, the sight of huge and shapeless walls. I cursed the old house for its lack of electricity. Fear might be eased in blazing lamplight. As it was, the imperfect flickering of that tiny flame did nothing to allay my fears.

I wanted to go across the hall and see if Saul were all right. But I was afraid to open my door, imagining hideous apparitions lurking there in the blackness, hearing once more in my mind the ugly, viscid laughter. I hoped that Saul was so hopelessly under alcoholic influence that nothing short of an earthquake could awaken him.

And, though I yearned to be near him even if he were treating me faithlessly, I felt no courage whatsoever. And, quickly undressing, I hastened to my bed and buried my head beneath the blankets again.

# V

I woke suddenly, shivering and afraid. The bedclothes were gone from my body, the black silence as awful as it had been earlier in the night.

I reached for the blankets anxiously, my fingers groping for them. They had fallen from the edge of the bed. I rolled on my side hurriedly and reached down, my fingers recoiling as they came in contact with the icy floorboards.

Then, as I reached for the blankets, I saw the light beneath the door.

It remained in sight only the fragment of a second but I knew I had seen it. And, as it passed abruptly from my eyes, the throbbing began. My room seemed filled with the humming pulsations. I could feel the bed shaking beneath me and my skin growing taut and frigid; my teeth chattering together.

Then the light appeared again and I heard the sound of bare feet and knew it was Saul walking in the night.

Driven more by fear for his safety than by courage, I threw my legs over the side of the bed and padded to the door, shuddering at the iciness of the flooring beneath my soles.

Slowly I opened the door, my body held tight in anticipation of what I might see.

But the hall was pitch black and I walked out and over to the door of Saul's room, listening to see if I could hear the sound of his breathing. But before I could judge anything, the hall below was suddenly illumined with that unearthly blue glow and I turned and rushed, again instinctively, to the head of the stairs and stood there clutching the old banister, staring down.

Below, an aura of intense brilliant blue light was passing through the hall moving in the direction of the living room.

My heart leaped! Saul was following it, arms ahead of him in the familiar pose of the somnambulist, his eyes staring ahead and glittering in the shapeless blue effulgence.

I tried to call his name but found that my voice could make no utterance. I tried to move for the stairs to wrest my Saul away from this terror. But a wall, invisible in the blackness, held me back. It grew close and airless. I struggled violently but it was to no avail. My muscles were strengthless against the horrible, impossible power that clutched me.

Then, suddenly, my nostrils and brain were assaulted by a pungent, sickly odor that made my senses reel. My throat and stomach burned with almost tangible fire. The darkness grew more intense. It seemed to cling to me like hot, black mud, constricting my chest so that I could hardly breathe. It was like being buried alive in a black oven, my body bound and rebound with heavy grave wrappings. I trembled, sobbing and ineffectual.

Then, abruptly, it all passed and I stood there in the cold hallway soaked with perspiration, weak from my frantic efforts. I tried to move but could not, tried to remember Saul, but was incapable of preventing the thought of him from slipping from my numbed brain. I shivered and turned to go back to my room but, at the first step, my legs buckled and I pitched forward heavily on the floor. The icy surface of it pressed against my flesh and, my body wracked by shivering, I lost consciousness.

When my eyes opened again I still lay crumpled on the cold floor.

I rose to a sitting position, the hall before my eyes wavering in alternate tides of light and darkness. My chest felt tight and a remorseless chill gripped my body. I pulled myself up to a bent-over stance and staggered to Saul's room, a cough burning in my throat as I stumbled across the floor and against his bed.

He was there and looked emaciated. He was unshaved and the dark wiry growth on his skin seemed like some repugnant growth. His mouth was open and emitting sounds of exhausted slumber and his smooth, white chest rose and fell with shallow movements.

He made no motion as I tugged weakly at his shoulder. I spoke his name and was shocked at the hoarse, grating sound of my own voice. I spoke it again, and he stirred with a grumble and opened one eye to look at me.

"I'm sick," I muttered, "Saul, I'm sick."

He rolled on one side, turning on his back to me. A sob of anguish tore at my throat.

"Saul!"

He seemed to snap his body around insanely then, his hands clenched into bony, white fists at his sides.

"Get out of here!" he screamed." "Leave me alone or I'll kill you!"

The body-shaking impact of his words drove me back from the bed to where I stood dumbly staring at him, breath stabbing at my throat. I saw him toss his body back over as if he wanted to break it. And I heard him mutter to himself miserably, "*Why does the day have to last so long?*"

A spasm of coughing struck me then and, my chest aching with fiery pains, I struggled back to my own room and got into bed with the movements of an old man. I fell back on the pillow and pulled up the blankets, then lay there shivering and helpless.

There I slept all day in spasmodic periods offset by waking moments of extreme pain. I was unable to rise to get myself food or water. All I could do was lie there, shaking and weeping. I felt beaten as much by Saul's cruelty to me as by the physical suffering. And the pain in my body was extremely severe. So much so that during one seizure of coughing it was so awful I began to cry like a child, hitting the mattress with weak, ineffective fists and kicking my legs deliriously.

Yet, even then, I think I wept for more than the pain. I wept for my only brother who loved me not.

It seemed that night came more swiftly than I had ever seen it come before. I lay alone in the darkness praying through mute lips that no harm should come to him.

I slept a while and then, abruptly, I was awake, staring at the light beneath the door, hearing the high-pitched humming in my ears. And I realized in that moment that Saul still loved me but that the house had corrupted his love.

And from this knowledge came resolution, from despair I gained amazing heart. I struggled to my feet and swayed there dizzily until the streaks before my eyes dispersed. Then I put on my robe and slippers, went to the door and threw it open.

What made things happen as they did I cannot say. Perhaps it was my feeling of courage that caused the black obstruction in the hall to melt before me. The house was trembling with the vibrations and the humming. Yet they seemed to lessen as I moved down the stairway and, all of a sudden, the blue light vanished from the living room and I heard loud and furious rumblings there.

When I entered, the room was in its usual order. A candle was burning on the mantel. But my eyes were riveted to the center of the floor.

Saul stood there, half naked and motionless, his body poised as though he were dancing, his eyes fastened to the portrait.

I spoke his name sharply. His eyes blinked and, slowly, his head turned to me. He didn't seem to comprehend my presence there for, suddenly, his glance flew about the room and he cried out in despairing tones:

"Come back! Come back!"

I called his name again and he stopped looking around but directed his gaze at me. His face was gaunt and cruelly lined in the flickerign candlelight. It was the face of a lunatic. He gnashed his teeth together and started to move toward me.

"I'll kill you," he muttered in liquid tones, "I'll *kill* you."

I backed away.

"Saul, you're out of your mind. You don't..."

I could say no more for he rushed at me, his hands extended as if he would clutch at my throat. I tried to step aside but he grabbed hold of my robe and pulled me against him.

We began to struggle, I begging him to throw off this terrible spell he was under, he panting and gnashing his teeth. My head was being shaken from side to side and I saw our monstrous shadows heaving on the walls.

Saul's grip was not his own. I have always been stronger than he but, at that moment, his hands seemed like cold iron.

I began to choke and his face blurred before my eyes. I lost balance and we both fell heavily to the floor. I felt the prickly rug against my cheek, his cold hands tightening on my throat.

Then my hand came in contact with something cold and hard. It was the tray I had dropped the night before, I realized. I gripped it and, realizing that he was out of his mind and meant to kill me, I picked it up and drove it across his head with all the power I had remaining.

It was a heavy metal tray and Saul sank to the floor as if struck dead, his hands slipping from my bruised throat. I struggled up, gasping for breath, and looked at him.

Blood was running from a deep gash in his forehead where the edge of the tray had struck.

"Saul!" I screamed, horrified at what I'd done.

Frantically I leaped up and rushed to the front door. As I flung it open I saw a man walking by in the street. I ran to the porch railing and called to him.

"Help!" I cried. "Call an ambulance!"

The man lurched and looked over at me with startled fright.

"For God's sake!" I beseeched him. "My brother has struck his head! Please call an ambulance!"

For a long moment he stared at me, open-mouthed, then broke into a nervous flight up the street. I called after him but he would not stop to listen. I was certain he would not do as I'd asked.

As I turned back, I saw my bloodless face in the hall mirror and realized with a start that I must have frightened the wits out of the man. I felt weak and afraid again, the momentary strength sapped from me. My throat was dry and raw, my stomach on edge. I was barely able to walk back to the living room on trembling stalks of legs.

I tried to lift Saul to a couch but dead weight was too much for me and I sank to my knees beside him. My body slumped forward and, half crouched, half lay by the side of my brother. The harsh sound of my breathing was the only sound I could hear. My left hand stroked Saul's hair absently and quiet tears flowed from my eyes.

I cannot say how long I had been there when the throbbing began again; as if to show me that it hadn't really gone away.

I still crouched there like a dead thing, my brain almost in coma. I could feel my heart beating like some old clock in my chest, the dull-edged and muffled pendulum hitting against my ribs with a lifeless rhythm. All sound registered with similar force, the clock on the mantel, my heart and the endless throbbing; all blending into one horrible beat that became a part of me, that became *me*. I could sense myself sinking deeper and deeper as a drowning man slips helplessly beneath the silent waters.

Then I thought I heard a tapping of feet through the room, the rustling of skirts and, far off, a hollow laughter of women.

I raised my head abruptly, my skin tight and cold.

A figure in white stood in the doorway.

It began to move toward me and I rose with a strangled cry on my lips only to collapse into darkness.

## VI

What I had seen had been not a ghost but an interne from the hospital. The man I had called in the street had, apparently, done what I'd asked. It will give some indication of the state I was in when I reveal that I heard neither the ringing of the front doorbell not the pounding of the interne's fist on the half-open door. Indeed, had the door not been open, I am certain that I would be dead now.

They took Saul to the hospital to have his head cared for. There being nothing wrong with me but nervous exhaustion, I remained in the house. I had wanted to go with Saul, but was told that the hospital was overcrowded and I would do more good by staying home in bed.

I slept late the next morning, rising about eleven. I went downstairs and had a substantial breakfast, then returned to my room and slept a few hours more. About two, I had some lunch. I planned to leave the house well before darkness to make sure nothing further happened to me. I could find a room in a hotel. It was clear that we would have to desert the place regardless of whether we sold it or not. I anticipated some trouble with Saul on that point but made up my mind to stand firm on my decision.

About five o'clock I dressed and left my room, carrying a small bag for the night. The day was almost gone and I hurried down the stairs, not wishing to remain in the house any longer. At the bottom of the staircase I stepped across the entry hall and closed my hand over the door knob.

The door would not open.

At first I would not allow myself to believe this. I stood there tugging, trying to combat the cold numbness that was spreading itself over my body. Then I dropped my bag and pulled at the knob with both hands but to no avail. It was as securely fastened as the cabinet door in the kitchen.

Suddenly, I turned from the door and ran into the living room but all the windows were jammed fast into their frames. I looked around the room, whimpering like a child, feeling unspoken hate for myself for letting myself be trapped again. I cursed loudly and, as I did, a cold wind lifted the hat from my head and hurled it across the floor.

Abruptly, I placed my shaking hands over my eyes and stood there trembling violently, afraid of what might happen any second, my heart hammering against my chest. The room seemed to chill markedly and I heard that grotesque humming noise again that came as if from another world. It sounded like laughter to me, laughter that mocked me for my poor, feeble efforts to escape.

Then, with equal suddenness, I remembered Saul again, remembered that he needed me and I pulled away my hands from my eyes and screamed aloud,

"Nothing in this house can harm me!"

Sudden cessation of the sound gave me added courage. If

my will could successfully defy the ungodly powers of the place, then perhaps it could also destroy them. If I went upstairs, if I slept in Saul's bed, then I too would know what he had experienced and thus be enabled to help him.

I felt no lack of confidence in my will to resist, never once stopping to think that my ideas might not be my own.

Quickly, two steps at a time, I rushed up the stairs and into my brother's room. There I quickly removed my hat, overcoat and suitcoat, loosened my tie and collar and sat down on the bed. Then, after a moment, I lay down and looked up at the darkening ceiling. I tried to keep my eyes open but, still fatigued, I soon fell asleep.

It seemed only a moment before I was fully awake, my body tingling with sensations of not unpleasant character. I could not understand the strangeness of it. The darkness seemed alive. It shimmered under my gaze as I lay there, warm with a heat that betokened sensualism although there was hardly any apparent cause for such a feeling.

I whispered Saul's name without thinking. Then the thought of him was taken from my brain as if invisible fingers had plucked it away.

I remember rolling over and laughing to myself, behavior most extraordinary if not unseemly for a person of my steady inclinations. The pillow felt like silk against my face and my senses began to fade. The darkness crept over me like warm syrup, soothing my body and mind. I muttered senselessly to myself, feeling as if my muscles were sucked dry of all energy, heavy as rock and lethargic with a delicious exhaustion.

Then, when I had almost slipped away, I felt another presence in the room. To my incredulous realization, it was not only familiar to me but I had absolutely no fear of it. Only an inexplicable sense of languorous expectation.

Then she came to me, the girl in the portrait.

I stared at the blue haze about her for only a moment for this quickly faded and, in my arms, was a vibrantly warm body. I remember no one feature of her behavior for everything was lost in overall sensation, a sensation mixed of excitement and revulsion, a sense of hideous yet overpowering rapacity. I hung suspended in a cloud of ambivalence, my soul and body corroded with unnatural desire. And in my mind and echoing on my tongue I spoke a name over and over again.

The name *Clarissa*.

How can I judge the number of sick, erotic moments I spent there with her? Sense of time completely vanished from the scheme of things. A thick giddiness enveloped me. I tried to fight it but it was no use. I was consumed as my brother Saul had been consumed by this foul presence from the grave of night.

Then, in some inconceivable fashion, we were no longer on the bed but downstairs, whirling about in the living room dancing wildly and closely. There was no music, only that incessant, beating rhythm I had heard those nights before. Yet now it seemed like music to me as I spun about the floor holding in my arms the ghost of a dead woman, entranced by her stunning beauty yet, at the same time, repelled by my uncontrollable hunger for her.

Once I closed my eyes for a second and felt a terrible coldness crawling in my stomach. But when I opened them it was gone and I was happy once more. *Happy?* It seems hardly the word now. Say rather hypnotized, torpid, my brain a numbed vessel of flesh unable to remove me one iota from this clutching spell.

Dancing went on and on. The floor was filled with couples. I am sure of that and yet I recall no aspect of their dress or form. All I remember is their faces, white and glistening, their eyes dull and lifeless, their mouths hanging open like dark, bloodless wounds.

Around and around and then a man with a large tray standing in the hallway arch and sudden immersion in the dark; empty and still.

## VII

I awoke with a sense of complete exhaustion.

I was soaked with perspiration, dressed only in my bottom undergarment. My clothes lay scattered across the floor, apparently thrown about in a frenzy. The bedclothes also lay in disordered heaps on the floor. From all appearances, I had gone insane the night before.

The light from the window annoyed me for some reason and, quickly, I shut my eyes, reluctant to believe it was morning again. I turned over onto my stomach and put my head beneath the pillow. I could still remember the enticing odor of her hair. The memory of it made my body shudder with odious craving.

Then a warmth began to cover my back and I raised myself up with a muttering frown. The sunlight was streaming through the windows onto my back. With a restless movement I pushed myself up, threw my legs over the side of the bed and got up to draw the shades.

It was a little better without the glare. I threw myself on the bed again, closed my eyes tightly and crowded the pillow over my head. I felt the light.

It sounds incredible, I know, but I felt it as surely as do certain creeper plants that climb towards the light without ever seeing it. And, in feeling light, I yearned all the more for darkness. I felt like some nocturnal creature somehow forced into brightness, repelled and pained by it.

I sat on the bed and looked around, a sound of unremitting complaint in my throat. I bit my lips, clenched and unclenched my hands, wanting to strike out violently at something, at anything. I found myself standing over an unlit candle, blowing sharply on it. I knew, even then, the senselessness of the act and yet I did it nevertheless, trying, inanely, to make an invisible flame go out so that night could return through its dark roads. Bringing back Clarissa.

*Clarissa.*

A clicking sound filled my throat and my body positively

writhed. Not in pain or pleasure but in a combination of the two. I put my brother's robe over my body and wandered out into the silent hallway. There were no physical wants, no hunger, thirst, or other needs. I was a detached body, a comatose slave to the tyranny which had shackled me and now refused to let me go.

I stood at the head of the stairway, listening intently, trying to imagine her gliding up to meet me, warm and vibrant in her mist of blue. *Clarissa.* I closed my eyes quickly, my teeth grated together and, for a split second, I felt my body stiffen with fright. For a moment I was returned to myself.

But then, in another breath, I was enslaved again. I stood there, feeling myself a part of the house, as much a portion of it as the beams or the windows. I breathed its breath, felt its soundless heartbeat in my own. I became at one with an inanimate body, knowing its past life, sensing the dead hands that had curled their fingers on the arms of the chairs, on banisters, on doorknobs, hearing the labored tread of invisible footsteps moving through the house, the laughter of long-consumed humor.

If, in those moments, I lost my soul, it became a part of the emptiness and stillness that surrounded me, an emptiness I could not sense nor a stillness feel for being drugged. Drugged with the formless presence of the past. I was no longer a living person. I was dead in all but those bodily functions which kept me from complete satisfaction.

Quietly, and without passion, the thought of killing myself drifted through my mind. It was gone in a moment but its passage had stirred no more in me than apathetic recognition. My thoughts were on the life beyond life. And present existence was no more than a minor obstruction which I could tumble with the slightest touch of razored steel, the minutest drop of poison. I had become the master of life for I could view its destruction with the most complete apathy.

Night. Night! When would it come? I heard my voice, thin and hoarse, crying out in the silence.

"Why does the day have to last so long!"

The words shocked me backed again, for Saul had spoken

them. I blinked, looked around me as if just realizing where I was. What was this terrible power over me? I tried to break its hold but, in the very effort, slipped back again.

To find myself once more in that strange coma which suspends the very ill in that slender portion of existence between life and death. I was hanging on a thread over the pit of everything that was hidden to me before. Now I could see and hear and the power to cut the thread was in my hands. I could let myself hang until the strands parted one by one and lowered me slowly down. Or I could wait until driven beyond endurance, then end it suddenly, cut myself loose and plunge down into the darkness; that signal darkness where she and hers remained always. Then I would have her maddening warmth. Maybe it was her coldness. Her comfort then. I could pass eternal moments with her and laugh at the robot world.

I wondered if it would help to get dead drunk and lose all consciousness till night.

I descended the stairs on unfeeling legs and sat for a long time before the mantel looking up at her. I had no idea what time it was nor did I care. Time was relative, even forgotten. I neither knew of it nor cared about it. Had she smiled at me then? Yes, her eyes glowed, how they glowed in the dimness. That smell again. Not pleasant yet something excitingly musky and pungent about it.

What was Saul to me? The idea filled my mind. He was no relation of mine. He was a stranger from another society, another flesh, another life. I felt complete dispassion toward him. You hate him, said the voice in my mind.

That was when it all collapsed like a flimsy house of cards.

For those words caused such a rebellion in my innermost mind that, suddenly, my eyes were cleared as though scales had fallen from them. I looked about, my head snapping crazily. What in God's name was I doing, still here in the house?

With a shiver of angry fear I jumped to my feet and ran upstairs to dress. As I passed the hall clock I saw with a start that it was past three in the afternoon.

As I dressed, normal sensations returned one by one. I felt the cold floor beneath my bare feet, became aware of hunger and thirst, heard the deep silence of the house.

Everything flooded over me. I knew why Saul had wanted to die, why he loathed the day and waited for the night with such angry impatience. I could explain it to him now and he would understand because I had been through it myself.

And, as I ran down the stairs, I thought about the dead of Slaughter House, so outraged at their own inexplicable curse that they tried to drag the living down into their endless hell.

Over, over!—exulted my mind as I locked the front door behind me and started through the misty rain to the hospital.

I did not see the shadow behind me, crouching on the porch.

## VIII

When the woman at the hospital desk told me that Saul had been discharged two hours before my arrival, I was too stunned to speak. I clutched at the counter, staring at her, hearing myself tell her that she must be mistaken. My voice was hoarse, unnatural. The woman shook her head.

I sagged against the counter then, all the drive gone out of me. I felt very tired and afraid. A sob broke in my throat as I turned away and I saw people staring at me while I moved across the tile floor with unsteady motions. Everything seemed to swirl about me. I staggered, almost fell. Someone clutched my arm and asked me if I were all right. I muttered something in reply and pulled away from the person without even noting if it were a man or a woman.

I pushed out through the door and into the gray light. It was raining harder and I pulled up my coat collar. Where was he? The question burned in my mind and the answer to it came quickly, too quickly. Saul was back in the house. I felt sure of it.

The idea made me start running up the dark street toward the trolley-car tracks. I ran for endless blocks. All I remember is the rain driving against my face and the gray buildings floating by. There were no people in the streets and all the taxicabs were full. It was getting darker and darker.

My legs almost buckled and I was thrown against a lamppost and clung to it, afraid of falling into the streaming gutter.

An ugly clanging filled my ears. I looked up, then chased after the trolley car and caught it at the next block. I handed the conductor a dollar and had to be called back for my change. I stood hanging from a black strap, swaying back and forth with the motion of the car, my mind tormented by thoughts of Saul alone in that house of horror.

The warm, stale air of the car began to make me sick to the stomach. I could smell the raincoats and the wet clothes of the people caught in the rain as well as the smell of dripping umbrellas and packages soaked. I closed my eyes and stood there, teeth clenched, praying that I would get home before it was too late.

I got off the car at last and ran up the block as fast as I could. The rain sprayed over my face and ran into my eyes, almost blinding me. I slipped and went sprawling on the sidewalk, skinning my hands and knees. I pushed up with a whine, feeling the clothes soaked against me. I kept running wildly, only sensing the direction by instinct until I stopped and saw through the thick veil of rain, the house in front of me, high and dark.

It seemed to crawl over the ground toward me and clutch me to itself for I found myself standing and shivering on the wooden porch. I coughed and felt the chill through my flesh.

I tried the door. At first I could not believe it. It was still locked and Saul had no key! I almost cried in gratitude. I ran down from the porch. Where was he then? I had to find him. I started down the path.

Then, as surely as if I had been tapped on the shoulder I

whirled about and stared up at the porch. A flash of lightning illuminated the darkness and I saw the broken, jagged-edged window. My breath caught and I stared at it, my heart pounding like a heavy piston in my chest.

He *was* in there. Had she come already? Was he lying upstairs in bed smiling to himself in the blackness, waiting for her luminous self to come and envelop him?

I had to save him. Without hesitation I ran up on the porch and unlocked the door, leaving it wide open so that we could escape.

I moved across the rug and onto the steps. The house was quiet. Even the storm seemed apart from it. The rushing sound of the rain seemed to grow less and less distinct. Then I turned with a gasp as the front door slammed shut behind me.

I was trapped. The thought drove barbs of fear into me and I almost ran down to try and escape. But I remembered Saul and fought to quicken resolution. I had conquered the house once and I could do it again. I had to. For him.

I started up the stairs again. Outside the flashes of lightning were like false neon trying to invade the austerity of the house. I held onto the banister tightly, muttering beneath my breath to keep attention from degrading into fright, afraid to let the spell of the house beset me again.

I reached the door to my brother's room. There I stopped and leaned against the wall, eyes closed. What if I found him dead? I knew the sight would unnerve me. The house might defeat me then, taking me in that moment of utter despair and twisting my soul from my grip.

I would not let myself conceive of it. I would not allow myself the realization that without Saul life was empty, a meaningless travesty. He *was* alive.

Nervously, my hands numbed with fright, I pushed open the door. The room was a stygian cave. My throat contracted and I took a deep breath. I clenched tight fists at my sides.

"Saul?" I called his name softly.

The thunder roared and my voice disappeared beneath the swell. A flash of lightning brought a split second of daylight into the room and I looked around quickly, hoping to see him.

Then it was dark again and silent except for the endless rain falling on the windows and roof. I took another step across the rug, cautiously, my ears tense, trying to hear. Every sound made me start. I twitched and shuffled across the floor. Was he here? But he must be. If he were here in the house, this was the room he would be in.

"Saul?" I called, louder. "Saul, answer me."

I began to walk toward the bed.

Then the door slammed behind me and there was a rushing sound behind me in the darkness. I whirled to meet it. I felt his hand clamp on my arm.

"Saul!" I cried.

Lightning filled the room with hideous light and I saw his twisted white face, the candlestick held in his right hand.

Then he struck me a violent blow on the forehead, driving a wedge of agonizing pain into my brain. I felt his hand release me as I slumped to my knees and my face brushed against his bare leg as I fell forward. The last sound I heard before my mind fell into the darkness was laughing and laughing and laughing.

## IX

I opened my eyes. I was still lying on the rug. Outside it was raining even harder. The sound of it was like the crashing of a waterfall. Thunder still rolled in the sky and flashes of lightning made the night brilliant.

In one flash I looked at the bed. The sight of the covers and sheets all thrown about insanely made me push up. Saul was downstairs with *her*!

I tried to get to my feet but the pain in my head drove me back to my knees. I shook my head feebly, running trembling hands over my cheeks, feeling the gouged wound in my forehead, the dried blood which had trickled down across one temple. I swayed back and forth on my knees, moaning. I seemed to be back in that void again, struggling to regain my hold on life. The power of the house surrounded me. The power which I knew was her power. A cruel and malignant vitality which tried to drink out the life force from me and draw me down into the pit.

Then, once more, I remembered Saul, my brother, and the remembrance brought me back the strength I needed.

"No!" I cried out as if the house had told me I was now its helpless captive. And I pushed to my feet, ignoring the dizziness, stumbling through a cloud of pain across the room, gasping for breath. The house was throbbing and humming, filled with that obnoxious smell.

I ran drunkenly for the door, found myself running into the bed. I drew back with almost a snarl at the numbing pain in my shins. I turned in the direction of the door and ran again. I did not even hold my arms ahead of me and had no chance to brace myself when I ran into the door dizzily.

The excruciating pain of my nose being near broken caused a howl of agony to pass my lips. Blood immediately began gushing down across my mouth and I had to keep wiping it away. I jerked open the door and ran into the hall, feeling myself on the border of insanity. The hot blood kept running down across my chin and I felt it dripping and soaking into my coat. My hat had fallen off but I still wore my raincoat over my suit.

I was too bereft of perception to notice that nothing held me back at the head of the stairs. I half ran, half slid down the stairs, goaded on by that humming, formless laughter which was music and mockery. The pain in my head was terrible. Every downward step made it feel as if someone drove one more nail into my brain.

"Saul, Saul!" I cried out, running into the living room, gagging as I tried to call his name a third time.

The living room was dark, permeated with that sickly odor. It made my head reel but I kept moving. It seemed to thicken as I moved for the kitchen. I ran into the small room and leaned against the wall, almost unable to breathe, pin-points of light spinning before my eyes.

Then, as lightning illumined the room I saw the left cup-board door wide open and, inside, a large bowl filled with what looked like flour. As I stared at it, tears rolled down my cheeks and my tongue felt like dry cloth in my mouth.

I backed out of the kitchen choking for breath, feeling as if my strength were almost gone. I turned and ran into the living room, still looking for my brother.

Then, in another flash of lightning, I looked at her portrait. It was different and the difference froze me to the spot. Her face was no longer beautiful. Whether it was shadow that did it or actual change, her expression was one of vicious cruelty. The eyes glittered, there was an insane cast to her smile. Even her hands, once folded in repose, now seemed more like claws waiting to strike out and kill.

It was when I backed away from her that I stumbled and fell over the body of my brother.

I pushed up to my knees and stared down in the blackness. One flash of lightning after another showed me his white, dead face, the smile of hideous knowledge on his lips, the look of insane joy in his wide-open eyes. My mouth fell open and breath caught in me. It seemed as if my world was ending. I could not believe it was true. I clutched at my hair and whimpered, almost believing that in a moment, Mother would wake me from my nightmare and I would look across at Saul's bed, smile at his innocent sleep and lie down again secure with the memory of his dark hair on the white pillow.

But it did not end. The rain slapped frenziedly at the windows and thunder drove deafening fists against the earth.

I looked up at the portrait. I felt as dead as my brother. I did not hesitate. Calmly I stood and walked to the mantel. There were matches there. I picked up the box.

Instantly, she divined my thoughts for the box was torn from my fingers and hurled against the wall. I dove for it and was tripped by some invisible force. Those cold hands clutched at my throat. I felt no fright but tore them away with a snarl and dove for the matches again. Blood began running faster and I spat out some.

I picked up the box. It was torn away again, this time to burst and spray matches all over the rug. A great hum of anguish seemed to rock the house as I reached for a match. I was grabbed. I tore loose. I fell to my knees and slapped at the rug in the darkness as lightning ceased. My arms here held tightly. Something cold and wet ran around in my stomach.

With maniacal fury I pressed my teeth against a match I saw in the lightning and bit at the head. There was no rewarding flare. The house was trembling violently now and I heard rustlings about me as if she had called them all to fight me, to save their cursed existence.

I bit at another match. A white face stared at me from the rug and I spit blood at it. It disappeared. I tore one arm loose and grabbed a match. I jerked myself to the mantel and dragged the match across the rough wood. A speck of flame flared up in my fingers and I was released.

The throbbing seemed more violent now. But I knew it was helpless against flame. I protected the flame with my hand though, lest that cold wind come again and try to blow it out. I held the match against a magazine that was lying on a chair and it flared up. I shook it and the pages puffed into flame. I threw it down on the rug.

I went around in that light striking one match after another, avoiding the sight of Saul lying there. She had destroyed him but now I would destroy her forever.

I ignited the curtains. I started the rug to smoldering. I set fire to the furniture. The house rocked and a whistling sigh rose and ebbed like the wind.

At last I stood erect in the flaming room, my eyes riveted on the portrait. I walked slowly toward it. She knew my intentions for the house rocked even harder and a shrieking began that seemed to come from the walls. And I knew then that the house was controlled by her and that her power was in that portrait.

I drew it down from the wall. It shook in my very hands as if it were alive. With a shudder of repugnance I threw it on the flames.

I almost fell while the floor shuddered almost as if an earthquake were striking the land. But then it stopped and the portrait was burning and the last effect of her was gone. I was alone in an old burning house.

I did not want anyone to know about my brother. I did not want anyone to see his face like that.

So I lifted him and put him on the couch. I do not understand to this day how I could life him up when I felt so weak. It was a strength not my own.

I sat at his feet, stroking his hand until the flames grew too hot. Then I rose. I bent over him and kissed him on the lips for a last good-bye. And I walked from the house into the rain. And I never came back. Because there was nothing to ever come back for.

*This is the end of the manuscript. There seems no adequate evidence to ascribe the events recounted as true. But the following facts, taken from the city's police files, might prove of interest.*

*In 1901, the city was severely shocked by the most wholesale murder ever perpetrated in its history.*

*At the height of a party being held at the home of Mr. and Mrs. Marlin Slaughter and their daughter Clarissa, an unknown person poisoned the punch by placing a very large amount of arsenic in it. Everyone died. The case was never solved although various theories were put forth as to its solution. One thesis had it that the murderer was one of those who died.*

*As to the identity of this murderer, supposition had it that it was not a murderer but a murderess. Although nothing definite exists to go by, there are several testimonies which refer to "that poor child Clarissa" and indicate that the young woman had been suffering for some years from a severe mental aberration which her parents had tried to keep a secret from the neighbors and the authorities. The party in mention was supposed to have been planned to celebrate what her parents took for the recovery of her faculties.*

*As to the body of the young man later supposed to be in the wreckage, a thorough search has revealed nothing. It may be that the entire story is imagination, fabricated by the one brother in order to conceal the death of the other, said death probably being unnatural. Thus, the older brother knowing the story of the house tragedy may have used it for a fantastic evidence in his favor.*

*Whatever the truth, the older brother has never been heard of again either in this city or in any of the adjacent localities.*

*And that's the story. S.D.M.*

# Shock Wave

"I tell you there's something wrong with her," said Mr. Moffat.

Cousin Wendall reached for the sugar bowl.

"Then they're right," he said. He spooned the sugar into his coffee.

"They are *not*," said Mr. Moffat, sharply. "They most certainly are *not*."

"If she isn't working," Wendall said.

"She *was* working until just a month or so ago," said Mr. Moffat. "She was working *fine* when they decided to replace her the first of the year."

His fingers, pale and yellowed, lay tensely on the table. His eggs and coffee were untouched and cold before him.

"Why are you so upset?" asked Wendall. "She's just an organ."

"*She is more*," Mr. Moffat said. "She was in before the church was even finished. Eighty years she's been there. *Eighty*."

"That's pretty long," said Wendall, crunching jelly-smeared toast. "Maybe too long."

"There's nothing wrong with her," defended Mr. Moffat. "Leastwise, there never was before. That's why I want you to sit in the loft with me this morning."

"How come you haven't had an organ man look at her?" Wendall asked.

"He'd just agree with the rest of them," said Mr. Moffat, sourly. "He'd just say she's too old, too worn."

"Maybe she is," said Wendall.

"*She is not*." Mr. Moffat trembled fitfully.

"Well, I don't know," said Wendall, "she's pretty old though."

"She worked fine before," said Mr. Moffat. He stared into the blackness of his coffee. "The gall of them," he muttered. "Planning to get rid of her. The *gall*."

He closed his eyes.

"Maybe she knows," he said.

The clocklike tapping of their heels perforated the stillness in the lobby.

"This way," Mr. Moffat said.

Wendall pushed open the arm-thick door and the two men spiraled up the marble staircase. On the second floor, Mr. Moffat shifted the briefcase to his other hand and searched his keyring. He unlocked the door and they entered the musty darkness of the loft. They moved through the silence, two faint, echoing sounds.

"Over here," said Mr. Moffat.

"Yes, I see," said Wendall.

The old man sank down on the glass-smooth bench and turned the small lamp on. A wedge of bulb light forced aside the shadows.

"Think the sun'll show?" asked Wendall.

"Don't know," said Mr. Moffat.

He unlocked and rattled up the organ's rib-skinned top, then raised the music rack. He pushed the finger-worn switch across its slot.

In the brick room to their right there was a sudden hum, a mounting rush of energy. The air-gauge needle quivered across its dial.

"She's alive now," Mr. Moffat said.

Wendall gurnted in amusement and walked across the loft. The old man followed.

"What do you think?" he asked inside the brick room.

Wendall shrugged.

"Can't tell," he said. He looked at the turning of the motor. "Single-phase induction," he said. "Runs by magnetism.''

He listened. ''Sounds all right to me,'' he said.

He walked across the small room.

''What's this?'' he asked, pointing.

''Relay machines,'' said Mr. Moffat. ''Keep the channels filled with wind.''

''And this is the fan?'' asked Wendall.

The old man nodded.

''Mmm-hmm.'' Wendall turned. ''Looks all right to me,'' he said.

The stood outside looking up at the pipes. Above the glossy wood of the enclosure box, they stood like giant pencils painted gold.

''Big,'' said Wendall.

''She's *beautiful*,'' said Mr. Moffat.

''Let's hear her,'' Wendall said.

They walked back to the keyboards and Mr. Moffat sat before them. He pulled out a stop and pressed a key into its bed.

A single tone poured out into the shadowed air. The old man pressed a volume pedal and the note grew louder. It pierced the air, tone and overtones bouncing off the church dome like diamonds hurled from a sling.

Suddenly, the old man raised his hand.

''*Did you hear*?'' he asked.

''Hear what?''

''It *trembled*,'' Mr. Moffat said.

As people entered the church, Mr. Moffat was playing Bach's chorale-prelude *Aus der Tiefe rufe ich* (From the Depths, I cry). His fingers moved certainly on the manual keys, his spindling shoes walked a dance across the pedals; and the air was rich with moving sound.

Wendall leaned over to whisper, ''There's the sun.''

Above the old man's gray-wreathed pate, the sunlight came filtering through the stained-glass window. It passed across the rack of pipes with a mistlike radiance.

Wendall leaned over again.

"Sounds all right to me," he said.

"*Wait*," said Mr. Moffat.

Wendall grunted. Stepping to the loft edge, he looked down at the nave. The three-aisled flow of people was branching off into rows. The echoing of their movements scaled up like insect scratchings. Wendall watched them as they settled in the brown-wood pews .Above and all about them moved the organ's music.

"*Sssst.*"

Wendall turned and moved back to his cousin.

"What is it?" he asked.

"*Listen.*"

Wendall cocked his head.

"Can't hear anything but the organ and the motor," he said.

"That's *it*," the old man whispered. "*You're not supposed to hear the motor.*"

Wendall shrugged. "So," he said.

The old man wet his lips. "I think it's starting," he murmured.

Below, the lobby doors were being shut. Mr. Moffat's gaze fluttered to his watch propped against the music rack, thence to the pulpit where the Reverend had appeared. He made of the chorale-prelude's final chord a shimmering pyramid of sound, paused, then modulated, *mezzo forte*, to the key of G. He played the opening phrase of the Doxology.

Below, the Reverend stretched out his hands, palms up, and the congregation took its feet with a rustling and crackling. An instant of silence filled the church. Then the singing began.

Mr. Moffat led them through the hymn, his right hand pacing off the simple route. In the third phrase an adjoining key moved down with the one he pressed and an alien dissonance blurred the chord. The old man's fingers twitched; the dissonance faded.

"*Praise Father, Son and Holy Ghost.*"

The people capped their singing with a lingering amen.

Mr. Moffat's fingers lifted from the manuals, he switched the motor off, the nave remurmured with the crackling rustle and the dark-robed Reverend raised his hands to grip the pulpit railing.

"Dear Heavenly Father," he said, "we, Thy children, meet with Thee today in reverent communion."

Up in the loft, a bass note shuddered faintly.

Mr. Moffat hitched up, gasping. His gaze jumped to the switch (off), to the air-gauge needle (motionless), toward the motor room (still).

*"You heard that?"* he whispered.

"Seems like I did," said Wendall.

*"Seems?"* said Mr. Moffat tensely.

"Well . . ." Wendall reached over to flick a nail against the air dial. Nothing happened. Grunting, he turned and started toward the motor room. Mr. Moffat rose and tiptoed after him.

"Looks dead to me," said Wendall.

*"I hope so,"* Mr Moffat answered. He felt his hands begin to shake.

The offertory should not be obtrusive but form a staidly moving background for the clink of coins and whispering of bills. Mr. Moffat knew this well. No man put holy tribute to music more properly than he.

Yet, that morning...

The discords surely were not his. Mistakes were rare for Mr. Moffat. The keys resisting, throbbing beneath his touch like things alive; was that imagined? Chords thinned to flesh-less octaves, then, moments later, thick with sound; was it he? The old man sat, rigid, hearing the music stir unevenly in the air. Ever since the Responsive Reading had ended and he'd turned the organ on again, it seemed to possess almost a willful action.

Mr. Moffat turned to whisper to his cousin.

Suddenly, the needle of the other gauge jumped from *mezzo* to *forte* and the volume flared. The old man felt his stomach muscles clamped. His pale hands jerked from the keys and, for a second, there was only the muffled sound of ushers' feet and money falling into baskets.

Then Mr. Moffat's hands returned and the offertory murmured once again, refined and inconspicuous. The old man noticed, below, faces turning, tilting upward curiously and a jaded pressing rolled in his lips.

"Listen," Wendall said when the collection was over, "How do you *know* it isn't you?"

"Because it isn't," the old man whispered back. "It's *her*."

"That's crazy," Wendall answered. "Without you playing, she's just a contraption."

"No," said Mr. Moffat, shaking his head, "*no*. She's more."

"Listen," Wendall said, "you said you were bothered because they're getting rid of her,"

The old man grunted.

"So," said Wendall, "I think you're doing these things yourself, unconscious-like."

The old man thought about it. Certainly, she was an instrument; he knew that. Her soundings were governed by his feet and fingers, weren't they? Without them, she was, as Wendall had said, a contraption. Pipes and levers and static rows of keys; knobs without function, arm-long pedals and pressuring air.

"Well, what do you think?" asked Wendall.

Mr. Moffat looked down at the nave.

"Time for the Benediction," he said.

In the middle of the Benediction postlude, the *swell to great stop* pushed out and, before Mr. Moffat's jabbing hand had shoved it in again, the air resounded with a thundering of horns, the church air was gorged with swollen, trembling sound.

*"It wasn't me,"* he whispered when the postlude was over, *"I saw it move by itself."*

"Didn't see it," Wendall said.

Mr. Moffat looked below where the Reverend had begun to read the words of the next hymn.

*"We've got to stop the service,"* he whispered in a shaking voice.

"We can't do that," said Wendall.

"But something's going to happen, I know it," the old man said.

"What can happen?" Wendall scoffed. "A few bad notes is all."

The old man sat tensely, staring at the keys. In his lap his hands wrung silently together. Then, as the Reverend finished reading, Mr. Moffat played the opening phrase of the hymn. The congregation rose and, following that instant's silence, began to sing.

This time no one noticed but Mr. Moffat.

Organ tone possesses what is called "inertia," an impersonal character. The organist cannot change this tonal quality; it is inviolate.

Yet, Mr. Moffat clearly heard, reflected in the music, his own disquiet. Hearing it sent chills of prescience down his spine. For thirty years he had been organist here. He knew the workings of the organ better than any man. Its pressures and reactions were in the memory of his touch.

That morning, it was a strange machine he played on.

A machine whose motor, when the hymn was ended, would not stop.

"Switch it off again," Wendall told him.

"I *did,*" the old man whispered frightenedly.

*"Try it again."*

Mr. Moffat pushed the switch. The motor kept running. He pushed the switch again. The motor kept running. He clenched his teeth and pushed the switch a seventh time.

The motor stopped.

*"I don't like it,"* said Mr. Moffat faintly.

"Listen, I've seen this before," said Wendall. "When you push the switch across the slot, it pushes a copper contact across some porcelain. That's what joins the wires so the current can flow.

"Well, you push that switch enough times, it'll leave a copper residue on the porcelain so's the current can move across it. Even when the switch is off. I've seen it before."

The old man shook his head.

"She *knows,*" he said.

"That's *crazy*," Wendall said.

*"Is it?"*

They were in the motor room. Below, the Reverend was delivering his sermon.

"Sure it is," said Wendall. "She's an organ, not a person."

"I don't know any more," said Mr. Moffat hollowly.

"Listen," Wendall said, "You want to know what it probably is?"

"She knows they want her out of here," the old man said, "That's what it is."

"Oh, come on," said Wendall, twisting impatiently, "I'll tell you what it is. This is an old church—and this old organ's been shaking the walls for eighty years. Eighty years of that and walls are going to start warping, floors are going to start settling. And when the floor settles, this motor here starts tilting and wires go and there's arcing."

"Arcing?"

"Yes," said Wendall. "Electricity jumping across gaps."

"I don't see," said Mr. Moffat.

"All this here extra electricity gets into the motor," Wendall said. "There's electromagnets in these relay machines. Put more electricity into them, there," there'll be more force. Enough to cause those things to happen maybe."

"Even if it's so," said Mr. Moffat, "Why is she fighting me?"

"Oh, stop talking like that," said Wendall.

"But I know," the old man said, "I *feel.*"

"It needs repairing is all," said Wendall. "Come on, let's go outside. It's hot in here."

Back on his bench, Mr. Moffat sat motionless, staring at the keyboard steps.

Was it true, he wondered, that everything was as Wendall had said—partly due to faulty mechanics, partly due to him?

He mustn't jump to rash conclusions if this were so. Certainly, Wendall's explanations made sense.

Mr. Moffat felt a tingling in his head. He twisted slightly, grimacing.

Yet, there were these things which happened: the keys going down by themselves, the stop pushing out, the volume flaring, the sound of emotion in what should be emotionless. Was this mechanical defect; or was this defect on his part? It seemed impossible.

The prickling stir did not abate. It mounted like a flame. A restless murmur fluttered in the old man's throat. Beside him, on the bench, his fingers twitched.

Still, things might not be so simple, he thought. Who could say conclusively that the organ was nothing but inanimate machinery? Even if what Wendall had said were true, wasn't it feasible that these very factors might have given strange comprehension to the organ? Tilting floors and ruptured wires and arcing and overcharged electro-magnets — mightn't these have bestowed cognizance?

Mr. Moffat sighed and straightened up. Instantly, his breath was stopped.

The nave was blurred before his eyes. It quivered like a gelatinous haze. The congregation had been melted, run together. They were welded substance in his sight. A cough he heard was hollow detonation miles away. He tried to move but couldn't. Paralyzed, he sat there.

And it came.

It was not thought in words so much as raw sensation. It pulsed and tremored in his mind electrically. *Fear—Dread—Hatred*—all cruelly unmistakable.

Mr. Moffat shuddered on the bench. Of himself, there remained only enough to think, in horror—*She does know!* The rest was lost beneath overcoming power. It rose up higher, filling him with black contemplations. The church was gone, the congregation gone, the Reverend and Wendall gone. The old man pendulumed above a bottomless pit while fear and hatred, like dark winds, tore at him possessively.

"Hey, what's wrong?"

Wendall's urgent whisper jarred him back. Mr. Moffat blinked.

"What happened?" he asked.

"You were turning on the organ."

"Turning on—?"

"And *smiling,*" Wendall said.

There was a trembling sound in Mr. Moffat's throat. Suddenly, he was aware of the Reverend's voice reading the words of the final hymn.

*"No,"* he murmured.

"What is it?" Wendall asked.

*"I can't turn her on."*

"What do you mean?"

"I *can't.*"

"Why?"

"I don't know. I just—"

The old man felt his breath thinned as, below, the Reverend ceased to speak and looked up, waiting. No, thought Mr. Moffat, No, I *mustn't.* Premonition clamped a frozen hand on him. He felt a scream rising in his throat as he watched his hand reach forward and push the switch.

The motor started.

Mr. Moffat began to play. Rather, the organ seemed to play, pushing up or drawing down his fingers at its will. Amorphous panic churned the old man's insides. He felt an overpowering urge to switch the organ off and flee.

He played on.

He started as the singing began. Below, armied in their pews, the people sang, elbow to elbow, the wine-red hymnals in their hands.

*"No,"* gasped Mr. Moffat.

Wendall didn't hear him. The old man sat staring as the pressure rose. He watched the needle of the volume gauge move past *mezzo* toward *forte.* A dry whimper filled his throat. No, please, he thought, *please.*

Abruptly, the *swell to great* stop slid out like the head of some emerging serpent. Mr. Moffat thumbed it in desperately. The *swell unison* button stirred. The old man held it in;

he felt it throbbing at his finger pad. A dew of sweat broke out across his brow. He glanced below and saw the people squinting up at him. His eyes fled to the volume needle as it shook toward *grand crescendo.*

"Wendall, try to—!"

There was no time to finish. The *swell to great* stop slithered out again, the air ballooned with sound. Mr. Moffat jabbed it back. He felt keys and pedals dropping in their beds. Suddenly, the *swell unison* button was out. A peal of unchecked clamor filled the church. No time to speak.

The organ was alive.

He gasped as Wendall reached over to jab a hand across the switch. Nothing happened. Wendall cursed and worked the switch back and forth. The motor kept on running.

Now pressure found its peak, each pipe shuddering with storm winds. Tones and overtones flooded out in a paroxysm of sound. The hymn fell mangled underneath the weight of hostile chords.

"Hurry!" Mr Moffat cried.

"It won't go off!" Wendall shouted back.

Once more, the *swell to great* stop jumped forward. Coupled with the volume pedal, it clubbed the walls with dissonance. Mr. Moffat lunged for it. Freed, the *swell unison* button jerked out again. The raging sound grew thicker yet. It was a howling giant shouldering the church.

*Grand crescendo.* Slow vibrations filled the floors and walls.

Suddenly, Wendall was leaping to the rail and shouting, "Out! Get Out!"

Bound in panic, Mr. Moffat pressed at the switch again and again; but the loft still shook beneath him. The organ still galed out music that was no longer music but attacking sound.

"Get out!" Wendall shouted at the congregation. *"Hurry!"*

The windows went first.

They exploded from their frames as though cannon shells

had pierced them. A hail of shattered rainbow showered on the congregation. Women shrieked, their voices pricking at the music's vast ascension. People lurched from their pews. Sound flooded at the walls in tidelike waves, breaking and receding.

The chandeliers went off like crystal bombs.

"*Hurry!*" Wendall yelled.

Mr. Moffat couldn't move. He sat staring blankly at the manual keys as they fell like toppling dominoes. He listened to the screaming of the organ.

Wendall grabbed his arm and pulled him off the bench. Above them, two last windows were disintegrated into clouds of glass. Beneath their feet, they felt the massive shudder of the church.

"*No!*" The old man's voice was inaudible; but his intent was clear as he pulled his hand from Wendall's and stumbled backward toward the railing.

"*Are you crazy?*" Wendall leaped forward and grabbed the old man brutally. They spun around in battle. Below, the aisles were swollen. The congragation was a fear-mad boil of exodus.

"Let me go!" screamed Mr. Moffat, his face a bloodless mask. "I have to stay!"

"No, you don't!" Wendall shouted. He grabbed the old man bodily and dragged him from the loft. The storming dissonance rushed after them on the staircase, drowning out the old man's voice.

"You don't understand!" screamed Mr. Moffat. "*I have to stay!*"

Up in the trembling loft, the organ played alone, its stops all out, its volume pedals down, its motor spinning, its bellows shuddering, its pipe mouths bellowing and shrieking.

Suddenly, a wall cracked open. Arch frames twisted, grinding stone on stone. A jagged block of plaster crumbled off the dome, falling to the pews in a cloud of white dust. The floors vibrated.

Now the congregation flooded from the doors like water.

Behind their screaming, shoving ranks, a window frame broke loose and somersaulted to the floor. Another crack ran crazily down a wall. The air swam thick with plaster dust.

Bricks began to fall.

Out on the sidewalk, Mr. Moffat stood motionless staring at the church with empty eyes.

He was the one. It had been he. How could he have failed to know it? His fear, his dread, his hatred. His fear of being also scrapped, replaced; his dread of being shut out from the things he loved and needed; his hatred of a world that had no use for aged things.

It had been he who turned the overcharged organ into a maniac machine.

Now, the last of the congregation was out. Inside the first wall collapsed.

It fell in a clamorous rain of brick and wood and plaster. Beams tottered like trees, then fell quickly, smashing down the pews like sledges. The chandeliers tore loose, adding their explosive crash to the din.

Then, up in the loft, the bass notes began.

The notes were so low they had no audible pitch. They were vibrations in the air. Mechanically, the pedals fell, piling up a mountainous chord. It was the roar of some titanic animal, the thundering of a hundred, storm-tossed oceans, the earth sprung open to swallow every life. Floors buckled, walls caved in with crumbling roars. The dome hung for an instant, then rushed down and mangled half the nave. A monstrous cloud of plaster and mortar dust enveloped everything. Within its swimming opacity, the church, with a crackling, splintering, crashing, thundering explosion, went down.

Later, the old man stumbled dazedly across the sunlit ruins and heard the organ breathing like some unseen beast dying in an ancient forest.

## When the Waker Sleeps

If one flew over the city at this time of this day, which was like any other day in the year 3850, one would think all life had disappeared.

Sweeping over the rustless spires, one would search in vain for the sight of human activity. One's gaze would scan the great ribboned highways that swept over and under each other like the weave of some tremendous loom. But there would be no autocars to see; nothing but the empty lanes and the colored traffic lights clicking out their mindless progressions.

Dipping low and weaving in and out among the glittering towers, one might see the moving walks, the studied revolution of the giant street ventilators, hot in the winter and cool in summer, the tiny doors opening and closing, the park fountains shooting their methodical columns of water into the air.

Farther along, one would flit across the great open field on which the glossy spaceships stood lined before their hangars. Farther yet, one would catch sight of the river, the metal ships resting along shore, delicate froth streaming from their sterns caused by the never-ending operation of their vents.

Again, one would glide over the city proper, seeking some sign of life in the broad avenues, the network of streets, the painstaking pattern of dwellings in the living area, the metal fastness of the commercial section.

The search would be fruitless.

All movement below would be seen to be mechanical. And, knowing what city this was, one's eyes would stop the search for citizens and seek out those squat metal structures which stood a half mile apart. These circular buildings housed the never-resting machines, the humming geared servants of the city's people.

These were the machines that did all: cleared the air of impurities, moved the walks and opened the doors, sent their synchronized impulses into the traffic lights, operated the fountains and the spaceships, the river vessels and the ventilators.

These were the machines in whose flawless efficacy the people of the city placed their casual faith.

At the moment, these people were resting on their pneumatic couches in rooms. And the music that seeped from their wall speakers, the cool breezes that flowed from their wall ventilators, the very air they breathed—all these were of and from the machines, the unfailing, the trusted, the infallible machines.

Now there was a buzzing in ears. Now the city came alive.

There was a buzzing, buzzing.

From the black swirl of slumber, you heard it. You wrinkled up your classic nose and twitched the twenty neural rods that led to the highways of your extremities.

The sound bore deeper, cut through swaths of snooze and poked an impatient finger in the throbbing matter of your brain. You twisted your head on the pillow and grimaced.

There was no cessation. With stupored hand, you reached out and picked up the receiver. One eye propped open by dint of will, you breathed a weary mutter into the mouthpiece.

"Captain Rackley!" The knifing voice put your teeth on edge.

"Yes," you said.

"You will report to your company headquarters immediately!"

That swept away sleep and annoyance as a petulant old man brushes chessmen from his board. Stomach muscles drew into play and you were sitting. Inside your noble chest, that throbbing meat ball, source of blood velocity, saw fit to swell and depress with marked emphasis. Your sweat glands engaged in proper activity, ready for action, danger, heroism.

"Is it . . . ?" you started.

"Report immediately!" the voice crackled, and there was a severe click in your ear.

You, Justin Rackley, dropped the receiver—plunko—in its cradle and leaped from bed in a shower of fluttering bedclothes.

You raced to your wardrobe door and flung it open. Plunging into the depths, you soon emerged with your skintight pants, the tunic for your forty-two chest. You donned said trousers and tunic, flopped upon a nearby seat and plunged your arches into black military boots.

And your face reflected oh-so-grim thoughts. Combing out your thick blond hair, you were sure you knew what the emergency was.

The Rustons! They were at it again!

Awake now, you wrinkled your nose with concious aplomb. The Rustons made revolting food for thought with their twelve legs, sign of alien progenitors, and their exudation of foul reptilian slime.

As you scurried from your room, leaped across the balustrade and down the stairs, you wondered once again where these awful Rustons had originated, what odious interbreeding produced their monster race. You wondered where they lived, where proliferated their grisly stock, held their meetings of war, began the upward slither to those great Earth fissures from which they massed in attack.

With nothing approaching answers to these endless questions, you ran out of the dwelling and flew down the steps to your faithful autocar. Sliding in, pushing buttons, levers, pedals, what have you, you soon had it darting through the streets toward the broad highway that led to headquarters.

At this time of day, naturally, there were very few people about. In point of fact you saw none. It was only a few minutes later, when you turned sharply and zoomed up the ramp to the highway, that you saw the other autocars whizzing toward the tower five miles distant. You guessed, and were correct in guessing, that they were fellow officers, all similarly ripped from slumber by mobilization.

Buildings flew past as you pushed pedals deeper into their cavities, your face always grim, alive to danger, grand warrior! True, you were not averse to the chance for activity after a month of idleness. But the circumstances *were* slightly distasteful. To think of the Rustons made a fellow shudder, eh?

What made them pour from their unknown pits? Why did they seek to destroy the machines, let the acid canker of their ooze eat through metal, make the teeth fall off the gears like petals off a dying flower? What was their purpose? Did they mean to ruin the city? Govern its inhabitants? Or slaughter them? Ugly questions, questions without answers.

Well, you thought as you drove into headquarters parking area, thank heaven the Rustons had only managed to get at a few of the outer machines, yours blessedly not included.

They, at least, had no more idea than you where the Great Machine was, that fabulous fountainhead of energy, driver of all machines.

You slid the seat of your military trousers across the seat of the autocar and jumped out into the wide lot. Your black boots clacked as you ran toward the entrance. Other officers were getting out of autocars, too, running across the area. None of them said anything; they all looked grim. Some of them nodded curtly at you as you all stood together in the rising elevator. Bad business, you thought.

With a tug at the groin, the door gave a hydraulic gasp and opened. You stepped out and padded silently down the hall to the high-ceilinged briefing room.

Already the room was almost filled. The young men, invariably handsome and muscular, stood in gregarious formations, discussing the Rustons in low voices. The gray soundproof walls sucked in their comments and returned dead air.

The men gave you a look and a nod when you entered, then

returned to their talking. Justin Rackley, captain, that's you, sat down in a front seat.

Then you looked up. The door to Upper Echelons was jerked open. The General came striding through, a sheaf of papers in his square fist. *His* face was grim, too.

He stepped up on the rostrum and slapped the papers on the thick table which stood there. Then he plumped down on the edge of it and kicked his boot against one of its legs until all your fellow officers had broken up their groups and hurriedly taken seats. With silence creeping over all heads, he pursed his lips and banged a palm on the table surface.

"Gentlemen," he said with that voice which seemed to issue from an ancient tomb, "once more the city lies in grave danger."

He then paused and looked capable of handling all emergencies. You hoped that someday you might be General and look capable of handling all emergencies. No reason why not, you thought.

"I will not take up precious time," the General went on, taking up precious time. "You all know your positions, you all know your responsibilities. When this briefing is concluded, you will report to the arsenal and draw out your ray guns. Always remember that the Rustons must not be allowed to enter the machinery and live. Shoot to kill. The rays are *not* harmful, repeat, *not* harmful to the machinery."

He looked over you eager young men.

"You also know," he said, "the dangers of Ruston poisoning. For this reason, that the slightest touch of their stingers can lead to abysmal agonies of death, you will be assigned, as you also know, a nurse trained in the combating of systemic poisons. Therefore, after leaving the arsenal, you will report to the Preventive Section."

He winked, a thoroughly out-of-place wink.

"And remember," he said, with a broad roll of import in his voice, "this is *war!* And *only* war!"

This, of course, brought on appreciative smiles, a smattering of leers and many unmilitary asides. Upon which the General snapped out of his brief role as chuckling confrere and returned to strict autocratic detachment.

"Once assigned a nurse, those of you whose machines are more than fifteen miles from the city will report to the spaceport, there to be assigned a spacecar. All of you will then proceed with utmost dispatch. Questions?"

No questions.

"I need hardly remind you," completed the General, "of the importance of this defense. As you are well aware, should Rustons penetrate our city, spread their ravaging to the core of our machine system, should they—heaven forfend!—locate the Great Machine, we may then expect nothing but the most merciless of butchery. The city would be undone, we would all be annihilated, Man would be overthrown."

The men looked at him with clenched fists, patriotism lurching through their brains like drunken satyrs, yours included, Justin Rackley.

"That is all," said the General, waving his hand. "Good shooting."

He jumped down from the platform and swept through the doorway, the door opening magically a split second before his imperious nose stood to shatter on its surface.

You stood up, muscles tingling. Onward! Save our fair city!

You stepped through the broken ranks. The elevator again, standing shoulder to shoulder with your comrades, a fluttering sense of hyperawareness coursing your healthy young body.

The arsenal room. Sound lost in the heavily padded interior. You, on line, grim-faced always, shuffling along, weapon bound. A counter; it was like an exchange market. You showed the man your identity card and he handed you a shiny ray gun and a shoulder case of extra ray pellets.

Then you passed through the door and scuffed down the rubberized steps to the Preventive Section. Corpuscles took a carnival ride through your veins.

You were fourth in line and she was fourth in line; that's how she was assigned to you.

You perused her contours, noting that her uniform, although similar to yours, somehow hung differently on her. This sidetracked martial contemplations for the nonce. *Zowie hoopla!*—your libido clapped its calloused hands.

"Captain Rackley," said the man, "this is Miss Lieutenant Forbes. She is your only guarantee against death should you be stung by a Ruston. See that she remains close by at all times."

This seemed hardly an onerous commission and you saluted the man. You then exchanged a flicker of lids with the young lady and intoned a gruff command relative to departure. This roused the two of you to walk to the elevator.

Riding down in silence, you cast glances at her. Long, forgotten threnodies twitched into life in your revitalized brain. You were much taken by the dark ringlets that hung over her forehead and massed on her shoulders liked curled black fingers. Her eyes, you noted, were brown and soft as eyes in a dream. And why shouldn't they be?

Yet something lacked. Some retardation kept bringing you down from ethereal cogitation. Could it, you wondered, be duty? And, remembering what you were out to do, you suddenly feared again. The pink clouds marched away in military formation.

Miss Lieutenant Forbes remained silent until the spacecar which you were assigned was flitting across the sky beyond the outskirts of the city. Then, following your somewhat banal overtures regarding the weather, she smiled her pretty little smile and showed her pretty little dimples.

"I am but sixteen," she announced.

"Then this is your first time."

"Yes," she replied, gazing afar. "I am very frightened."

You nodded, you patted her knee with what you meant to be a parental manner, but which, posthaste, brought the crimson of modesty flaming into her cheeks.

"Just stay close to me," you said, trying hard for a double meaning. "I'll take care of you."

Primitive, but good enough for sixteen. She blushed more deeply.

The city towers flashed beneath. Far off, like a minute

button on the fringes of spiderweb, you saw your machine. You eased the wheel forward; the tiny ship dipped down and began a long glide toward Earth. You kept your eyes on the control board with strict attention, wondering about this strange sense of excitement running pell-mell through your body, not knowing whether it presaged combat fatigue of one sort or another.

This was war. The city first. Hola!

The ship floated down to and hovered over the machine as you threw on the air brakes. Slowly, it sank to the roof like a butterfly settling on a flower.

You threw off the switch, heart pounding, all forgotten but the present danger. Grabbing the ray gun, you jumped out and ran to the edge of the roof.

Your machine was beyond the perimeter of the city. There were fields about. Your keen eyes flashed over the ground.

There was no sign of the enemy.

You hurried back to the ship. She was still sitting inside watching you. You turned the knob and the communicator system spilled out its endless drones of information. You stood impatiently until the announcer spoke your machine number and said the Rustons were within a mile of it.

You heard her drawn-in breath and noted the upward cast of frightened eyes in your direction. You turned off the set.

"Come, we'll go inside," you said, holding the ray gun in a delightfully shaking hand. It was fun to be frightened. A fine sense of living dangerously. Wasn't that why you were here?

You helped her out. Her hand was cold. You squeezed it and gave her a half smile of confidence. Then, locking the door to the spacecar, to keep the foe out, you went down the stairs. As you entered the main room, your head was at once filled with the smooth hum of machinery.

Here, at this juncture of the adventure, you put down your ray gun and ammunition and explained the machinery to her. It is to be noted that you had no particular concern for the machinery as you spoke, being more aware of her proximity. Such charm, such youth, crying out for comfort.

You soon held her hand again. Then you had your arm around her lithesome waist and she was close. Something other than military defense planned itself in your mind.

Came the moment when she flicked up her drowsy lids and looked you smack-dab in the eye, as is the archaic literary passage. You found her violet eyes somewhat unbalancing. You drew her closer. The perfume of her rosy breath tied casual knots in your limbs. And yet there was still something holding you back.

*Swish! Slap!*

She stiffened and cried out.

The Rustons were at the walls!

You raced for the table upon which your ray gun rested. On the couch next to the table was your ammunition. You slung the case over your shoulder. She ran up to you and, sternly, you handed her the preventive case. You felt like the self-assured General when he was in a grim mood.

"Keep the needles loaded and handy," you said. "I may..."

The sentence died as another great slobbering Ruston slapped against the wall. The sound of its huge suckers slurped on the outside. They were searching for the machinery in the basement.

You checked the gun. It was ready.

"Stay here," you muttered. "I have to go down."

You didn't hear what she said. You dashed down the stairs and came bouncing out into the basement just as the first horror gushed over the edge of a window onto its metal floor like a stream of gravity-defying lava.

The row of blinking yellow eyes turned on you; your flesh crawled. The great brown-gold monstrosity began to scuttle across toward the machines with an oily squish. You almost froze in fear.

Then instinct came to the fore. You raised the gun quickly. A crackling, brilliantine-blue ray leaped from the muzzle, touched the scaly body and enveloped it. Screeching and the smell of frying oil filled the air. When the ray had dissipated, the dead Ruston lay black and smoking on the floor, its slime running across the welded seams.

You heard the sound of suckers behind. You whirled, blasted the second of the Rustons into greasy oblivion. Still another slid over the window edge and started toward you. Another burst from the gun and another scorched hulk lay twitching on the metal.

You swallowed a great lump of excitement in your throat, your head snapping around, your body leaping from side to side. In a second, two more of them were moving toward you. Two bursts of ray; one missed. The second monster was almost upon you before you burst it into flaming chunks as it reared up to plunge its black stingers in your chest.

You turned quickly, cried out in horror.

One Ruston was just slipping down the stairs, another swishing toward you, the long stingers aimed at your heart. You pressed the button. A scream caught in your throat.

You were out of pellets!

You leaped to the side and the Ruston fell forward. You tore open the case and fumbled with the pellets. One fell and shattered uselessly on the metal. Your hands were ice, they shook terribly. The blood pounded through your veins, your hair stood on end. You felt scared and amused.

The Ruston lunged again as you slid the pellet into the ray gun. You dodged again—not enough! The end of one stinger slashed through your tunic, laid open your arm. You felt the burning poison shoot into your system.

You pressed the button and the monster disappeared in a cloud of unguent smoke. The basement machinery was secure against attack—the Rustons had bypassed it.

You leaped for the stairway. You had to save the machines, save her, save yourself!

Your boots banged up the metal stairs. You lunged into the great room of machines and swept a glance around.

A gasp tore open your mouth. She was collapsed on a couch, sprawled, inert. A Ruston line of slime ran down the front of her swelling tunic.

You whirled and, as you did, the Ruston vanished into the

machinery, pushing its scaly body through the gear spaces. The slime dropped from its body and watery jaws. The machine stopped, started again, the racked wheels groaning.

The city! You leaped to the machine's edge and shot a blast from the ray gun into it! The brilliantine-blue ray licked out, missed the Ruston. You fired again. The Ruston moved too fast, hid behind the wheels. You ran around the machine, kept on firing.

You glanced at her. How long did the poison take? They never said. Already in your flesh, however, the burning had begun. You felt as if you were going up in flames, as if great pieces of your body were about to fall off.

You had to get an injection for yourself and her.

Still the Ruston eluded you. You had to stop and put another pellet in the gun. The interior began to whirl around you; you were overpoweringly dizzy. You pressed the button again and again. The ray darted into the machine.

You reeled around with a sob and tore open your collar. You could hardly breathe. The smell of the singed suet, of the rays, filled your head. You stumbled around the machine, shot out another ray at the fast-moving Ruston.

Then, finally, when you were about to keel over, you got a good target. You pressed the button, the Ruston was enveloped in flame, fell in molten bits beneath the machine, was swallowed up by the waste exhaust.

You dropped the ray gun and staggered over to her.

The hypodermics were on the table.

You tore open her tunic and jabbed a needle into her soft white shoulder, shudderingly injected the antidote into her veins. You stuck another into your own shoulder, felt the sudden coolness run through your flesh and your bloodstream.

You sank down beside her, breathing heavily and closing your eyes. The violence of activity had exhausted you. You felt as though you would have to rest a month after this. And, of course, you would.

She groaned. You opened your eyes and looked at her.

Your heavy breathing began again, but this time you knew where the excitement was coming from. You kept looking at her. A warm heat lapped at your limbs, caressed your heart. Her eyes were on you.

"I . . ." you said.

Then all holding back was ended, all doubt undone. The city, the Rustons, the machines—the danger was over and forgotten. She ran a caressing hand over your cheek.

"And when next you opened your eyes," finished the doctor, "you were back in this room."

Rackley laughed, his head quivering on the pillow, his hands twitching in glee.

"But my dear doctor," he laughed, "how fantastically clever of you to know everything. How*ever* do you do it, naughty man?"

The doctor looked down at the tall handsome man who lay on the bed, still shaking with breathless laughter.

"You forget," he said, "I inject you. Quite natural that I should know what happens then."

"Oh, quite! Quite!" cried Justin Rackley. "Oh, it was utterly, utterly fantastic. Imagine me!" He ran strong fingers over the swelling biceps of his arm. "*Me*, a hero!"

He clapped his hands together and deep laughter rumbled in his chest, his white teeth flashed against the glowing tan of his face. The sheet slipped, revealing the broad suppleness of his chest, the tightly ridged stomach muscles.

"Oh, dear me," he sighed. "Dear me, what *would* this dull existence be without your blessed injections to ease our endless boredom?"

The doctor looked coldly at him, his strong white fingers tightening into a bloodless fist. The thought plunged a cruel knife into his brain—this is the end of our race, the sorry peak of Man's evolution. This is the final corruption.

Rackley yawned and stretched his arms. "I must rest." He peered up at the doctor. "It was such a *fatiguing* dream."

He began to giggle, his great blond head lolling on the

pillow. His hands striking at the sheet as though he would die of amusement.

"Do tell me," he gasped, "what on earth have you in those utterly delightful injections? I've asked you so often."

The doctor picked up his plastic bag. "Merely a combination of chemicals designed to exacerbate the adrenals on one hand and, on the other, to inhibit the higher brain centers. In short," he finished, "a potpourri of intensification and reduction."

"Oh, you always say that," said Justin Rackley. "But it *is* delightful. Utterly, charmingly delightful. You will be back in a month for my next dream and my dream playback?"

The doctor blew out a weary gust of breath. "Yes," he said, making no effort to veil his disgust. "I'll be back next month."

"Thank heavens," said Rackley, "I'm done with that awful Ruston dream for another five months. Ugh! It's so frightfully vile! I like the pleasanter dreams about mining and transporting ores from Mars and the Moon, and the adventures in food centers. They're so much nicer. But . . ." His lips twitched. "*Do* have more of those pretty young girls in them."

His strong, weary body twisted in delight.

"Oh, *do*" he murmured, his eyes shutting.

He sighed and turned slowly and exhaustedly onto his broad, muscular side.

The doctor walked through the deserted streets, his face tight with the old frustration. Why? Why? His mind kept repeating the word.

Why must we continue to sustain life in the cities? For what purpose? Why not let civilization in its last outpost die as it means to die? Why struggle to keep such men alive?

Hundreds, thousands of Justin Rackleys—well-kept animals, mechanically bred and fed and massaged into fair and handsome form. Mechanically restrained, too, from physically turning into the fat white slugs that, mentally, they already were and would bodily resemble if left untended. Or die.

Why not let them? Why visit them every month, fill their veins with hypnotic drugs and sit back and watch them, one by one, go bursting into their dream worlds to escape boredom? Must he endlessly send his suggestions into their loosened brainways, fly them to planets and moons, crowd all forms of love and grand adventure into their mock-heroic dreams?

The doctor slumped tiredly and went into another dorm-building. More figures, strongly or beautifully made, passive on couches. More dream injections.

He made them, watched the figures stand and stumble to the wardrobes. Explorers' outfits this time, pith helmets and attractive shorts, snake boots and bared limbs. He stood at the window, saw them clamber into their autocars and drive away. He sat back and waited for them to return, knowing every move they would make, because he made them in his mind.

They would go out to the hydroponics tanks and fight off an invasion of Energy Eaters. Bigger than the Rustons and made of pure force, they threatened to suck the sustenance from the plants in the growing trays, the living, formless meat swelling immortally in the nutrient solutions. The Energy Eaters would be beaten off, of course. They always were.

Naturally. They were only dreams. Creatures of fantastic illusion, conjured in eager dreaming minds by chemical magic and dreary scientific incantation.

But what would all these Justin Rackleys say, these handsome and hopeless ruins of torpid flesh, if they found out how they were being fooled?

Found out that the Rustons were only mental fictions for objectifying simple rust and wear and converting them into fanciful monsters. Monsters which alone could feebly arouse the dim instinct for self-preservation which just barely existed in this lost race. Energy Eaters—beetles and spores and exhausted growth solutions. Mine Borers—vaporous beasties that had to be blasted out of the Lunar and Martian metal deposits. And others, still others, all of them threats to that which runs and feeds and renews a city.

What would all these Justin Rackleys say, these hand- discovery that each of them, in his "dreams," had done genuine manual work? That their ray guns were spray guns or grease guns or air hammers, their death rays no more than streams of lubrication for rusting machines or insecticides or liquid fertilizer?

What would they say if they found out how they were tricked into breeding with aphrodisiacs in the guise of anti-poison shots? How they, with no healthy interest in procreation, were drugged into furtherance of their spineless strain, a strain whose only function was to sustain the life-giving machines.

In a month he would return to Justin Rackley, *Captain* Justin Rackley. A month for rest, these people were so devoid of energy. It took a month to build up even enough strength to endure an injection of hypnotics, to oil a machine or tend a tray, and to bring forth one puny cell of life.

All for the machines, the city, for man...

The doctor spat on the immaculate floor of the room with the pneumatic couches.

The people were the machines, more than the machines themselves. A slave race, a detestable residue, hopeless, without hope.

Oh, how they would wail and swoon, he thought, getting grim pleasure in the notion, were they allowed to walk through the vast subterranean tunnel to the giant chamber where the Great Machine stood, that supposed source of all energy, and saw why they had to be tricked into working. The Great Machine had been designed to eliminate all human labor, tending the minor machines, the food plants, the mining.

But some wise one on the Control Council, centuries before, had had the wit to smash the Great Machine's mechanical brain. And now the Justin Rackleys would have to see, with their own unbelieving eyes, the rust, the rot, the giant twisted death of it. . . . But they wouldn't.

Their job was to dream of adventurous work, and work while dreaming.

For how long?

# Witch War

Seven pretty little girls sitting in a row. Outside, night, pouring rain—war weather. Inside, toasty warm. Seven overalled little girls chatting. Plaque on the wall saying: P.G. CENTER.

Sky clearing its throat with thunder, picking and dropping lint lightning from immeasurable shoulders. Rain hushing the world, bowing the trees, pocking earth. Square building, low, with one wall plastic.

Inside, the buzzing talk of seven pretty little girls.

"So I say to him— 'Don't give me *that*, Mr. High and Mighty.' So he says, 'Oh yeah?' And I say, 'Yeah!' "

"Honest, will I ever be glad when this thing's over. I saw the cutest hat on my last furlough. Oh, *what* I wouldn't give to wear it!"

"You too? Don't I *know* it! You just can't get your hair right. Not in *this* weather. Why don't they let us get rid of it?"

"*Men!* They make me sick."

Seven gestures, seven postures, seven laughters ringing thin beneath thunder. Teeth showing in girl giggles. Hands tireless, painting pictures in the air.

P.G. Center. Girls. Seven of them. Pretty. Not one over sixteen. Curls. Pigtails. Bangs. Pouting little lips—smiling, frowning, shaping emotion on emotion. Sparkling young eyes—glittering, twinkling, narrowing, cold or warm.

Seven healthy young bodies restive on wooden chairs. Smooth adolescent limbs. Girls—pretty girls—seven of them.

An army of ugly shapeless men, stumbling in mud, struggling along the pitchblack muddy road.

Rain a torrent. Buckets of it thrown on each exhausted man. Sucking sound of great boots sinking into oozy yellow-brown mud, pulling loose. Mud dripping from heels and soles.

Plodding men—hundreds of them—soaked, miserable, depleted. Young men bent over like old men. Jaws hanging loosely, mouth gasping at black wet air, tongues lolling, sunken eyes looking at nothing, betraying nothing.

Rest.

Men sink down in the mud, fall on their packs. Heads thrown back, mouths open, rain splashing on yellow teeth. Hands immobile—scrawny heaps of flesh and bone. Legs without motion—khaki lengths of worm-eaten wood. Hundreds of useless limbs fixed to hundreds of useless trunks.

In back, ahead, beside rumble trucks and tanks and tiny cars. Thick tires splattering mud. Fat treads sinking, tearing at mucky slime. Rain drumming wet fingers on metal and canvas.

Lightning flashbulbs without pictures. Momentary burst of light. The face of war seen for a second—made of rusty guns and turning wheels and faces staring.

Blackness. A night hand blotting out the brief storm glow. Wind-blown rain flitting over fields and roads, drenching trees and trucks. Rivulets of bubbly rain tearing scars from the earth. Thunder, lightning.

A whistle. Dead men resurrected. Boots in sucking mud again—deeper, closer, nearer. Approach to a city that bars the way to a city that bars the way to a . . .

An officer sat in the communication room of the P.G. Center. He peered at the operator, who sat hunched over the control board, phones over his ears, writing down a message.

The officer watched the operator. They are coming, he thought. Cold, wet and afraid they are marching at us. He shivered and shut his eyes.

He opened them quickly. Visions fill his darkened

pupils—of curling smoke, flaming men, unimaginable horrors that shape themselves without words or pictures.

"Sir," said the operator, "from advance observation post. Enemy forces sighted."

The officer got up, walked over to the operator and took the message. He read it, face blank, mouth parenthesized. "Yes," he said.

He turned on his heel and went to the door. He opened it and went into the next room. The seven girls stopped talking. Silence breathed on the walls.

The officer stood with his back to the plastic window. "Enemies," he said, "two miles away. Right in front of you."

He turned and pointed out the window. "Right out there. Two miles away. Any questions?"

A girl giggled.

"Any vehicles?" another asked.

"Yes. Five trucks, five small command cars, two tanks."

"That's too easy," laughed the girl, slender fingers fussing with her hair.

"That's all," said the officer. He started from the room. "Go to it," he added and, under his breath, "Monsters!"

He left.

"Oh, me," sighed one of the girls, "here we go again."

"What a bore," said another. She opened her delicate mouth and plucked out chewing gum. She put it under her chair seat.

"At least it stopped raining," said a redhead, tying her shoelaces.

The seven girls looked around at each other. *Are you ready?* said their eyes. *I'm ready, I suppose*. They adjusted themselves on the chairs with girlish grunts and sighs. They hooked their feet around the legs of their chairs. All gum was placed in storage. Mouths were tightened into prudish fixity. The pretty little girls made ready for the game.

Finally they were silent on their chairs. One of them took a deep breath. So did another. They all tensed their milky flesh and clasped fragile fingers together. One quickly scratched her head to get it over with. Another sneezed prettily.

"Now," said a girl on the right end of the row.

Seven pairs of beady eyes shut. Seven innocent little minds began to picture, to visualize, to transport.

Lips rolled into thin gashes, faces drained of color, bodies shivered passionatley. Their fingers twitching with concentration, seven pretty little girls fought a war.

The men were coming over the rise of a hill when the attack came. The leading men, feet poised for the next step, burst into flame.

There was no time to scream. Their rifles slapped down into the muck, their eyes were lost in fire. They stumbled a few steps and fell, hissing and charred, into the soft mud.

Men yelled. The ranks broke, They began to throw up their weapons and fire at the night. More troops puffed incandescently, flared up, were dead.

"Spread out!" screamed an officer as his gesturing fingers sprouted flame and his face went up in licking yellow heat.

The men looked everywhere. Their dumb terrified eyes searched for an enemy. They fired into the fields and woods. The shot each other. They broke into flopping runs over the mud.

A truck was enveloped in fire. Its driver leaped out, a two-legged torch. The truck went bumping over the road, turned, wove crazily over the field, crashed into a tree, exploded and was eaten up in blazing light. Black shadows flitted in and out of the aura of light around the flames. Screams rent the night.

Man after man burst into flame, fell crashing on his face in the mud. Spots of searing light lashed the wet darkness—screams—running coals, sputtering, glowing, dying—incendiary ranks—trucks cremated—tanks blowing up.

*A little blonde, her body tense with repressed excitement. Her lips twitch, a giggle hovers in her throat. Her nostrils dilate. She shudders in giddy fright. She imagines, imagines . . .*

A soldier runs headlong across a field, screaming, his eyes

insane with horror. A gigantic boulder rushes at him from the black sky.

His body is driven into the earth, mangled. From the rock edge, fingertips protrude.

The boulder lifts from the ground, crashes down again, a shapeless trip hammer. A flaming truck is flattened. The boulder flies again to the black sky.

*A pretty brunette, her face a feverish mask. Wild thoughts tumble through her virginal brain. Her scalp grows taut with ecstatic fear. Her lips draw back from clenching teeth. A gasp of terror hisses from her lips. She imagines, imagines . . .*

A soldier falls to his knees. His head jerks back. In the light of burning comrades, he stares dumbly at the white-foamed wave that towers over him.

It crashes down, sweeps his body over the muddy earth, fills his lungs with salt water. The tidal wave roars over the field, drowns a hundred flaming men, tosses their corpses in the air with thundering whitecaps.

Suddenly the water stops, flies into a million pieces and disintegrates.

*A lovely little redhead, hands drawn under her chin in tight bloodless fists. Her lips tremble, a throb of delight expands her chest. Her white throat contracts, she gulps in a breath of air. Her nose wrinkles with dreadful joy. She imagines, imagines . . .*

A running soldier collides with a lion. He cannot see in the darkness. His hands strike wildly at the shaggy mane. He clubs with his rifle butt.

A scream. His face is torn off with one blow of thick claws. A jungle roar billows in the night.

A red-eyed elephant tramples wildly through the mud, picking up men in its thick trunk, hurling them through the air, mashing them under driving black columns.

Wolves bound from the darkness, spring, tear at throats. Gorillas scream and bounce in the mud, leap at falling soldiers.

A rhinoceros, leather skin glowing in the light of living

torches, crashes into a burning tank, wheels, thunders into blackness, is gone.

Fangs—claws—ripping teeth—shrieks—trumpeting—roars. The sky rains snakes.

Silence. Vast brooding silence. Not a breeze, not a drop of rain, not a grumble of distant thunder. The battle is ended.

Gray morning mist rolls over the burned, the torn, the drowned, the crushed, the poisoned, the sprawling dead.

Motionless trucks—silent tanks, wisps of oily smoke still rising from their shattered hulks. Great death covering the field. Another battle in another war.

Victory—everyone is dead.

The girls stretched languidly. They extended their arms and rotated their round shoulders. Pink lips grew wide in pretty little yawns. They looked at each other and tittered in embarrassment. Some of them blushed. A few looked guilty.

Then they all laughed out loud. They opened more gum-packs, drew compacts from pockets, spoke intimately with schoolgirl whispers, with late-night dormitory whispers.

Muted giggles rose up fluttering in the warm room.

"Aren't we awful?" one of them said, powdering her pert nose.

Later they all went downstairs and had breakfast.

# First Anniversary

Just before he left the house on Thursday morning, Adeline asked him "Do I still taste sour to you?"

Norman looked at her reproachfully.

"Well, do I?"

He slipped his arms around her waist and nibbled at her throat.

"Tell me now," said Adeline.

Norman looked submissive.

"Aren't you going to let me live it down?" he asked.

"Well, you *said* it, darling. And on our first anniversary, too!"

He pressed his cheek to hers. "So I said it," he murmured. "Can't I be allowed a faux pas now and then?"

"You haven't answered me."

"Do you taste sour? Of course you don't." He held her close and breathed the fragrance of her hair. "Forgiven?"

She kissed the tip of his nose and smiled and, once more, he could only marvel at the fortune which had bestowed on him such a magnificent wife. Starting their second year of marriage, they were still like honeymooners.

Norman raised her face and kissed her.

"Be damned," he said.

"What's wrong? Am I sour again?"

"No." He looked confused. "Now I can't taste you at all."

"Now you can't taste her at all," said Dr. Phillips.

Norman smiled. "I know it sounds ridiculous," he said.

"Well, it's unique, I'll give it that," said Phillips.

"More than you think," added Norman, his smile grown a trifle labored.

"How so?"

"I have no trouble tasting anything else."

Dr. Phillips peered at him awhile before he spoke. "Can you smell her?" he asked then.

"Yes."

"You're sure."

"*Yes*. What's that got to do with — " Norman stopped. "You mean that the senses of taste and smell go together," he said.

Phillips nodded. "If you can smell her, you should be able to taste her."

"I suppose," said Norman, "But I can't."

Dr. Phillips grunted wryly. "Quite a poser."

"No ideas?" asked Norman.

"Not offhand," said Phillips, "though I suspect it's allergy of some kind."

Norman looked disturbed.

"I hope I find out soon," he said.

Adeline looked up from her stirring as he came into the kitchen. "What did Dr. Phillips say?"

"That I'm allergic to you."

"He didn't say that," she scolded.

"Sure he did."

"Be serious now."

"He said I have to take some allergy tests."

"He doesn't think it's anything to worry about, does he?" asked Adeline.

"No."

"Oh, good." She looked relieved.

"Good, nothing," he grumbled. "The taste of you is one of the few pleasures I have in life."

"You stop that." She removed his hands and went on stirring. Norman slid his arm around her and rubbed his nose on the back of her neck. "Wish I could taste you," he said.

"I like your flavor."

She reached up and caressed his cheek. "I love you," she said.

Norman twitched and made a startled noise.

"What's wrong?" she asked.

He sniffed. "What's that?" He looked around the kitchen. "Is the garbage out?" he asked.

She answered quietly. "Yes, Norman."

"Well something sure as hell smells awful in here. Maybe —" He broke off, seeing the expression on her face. She pressed her lips together and, suddenly, it dawned on him. "Honey, you don't think I'm saying—"

"Well, *aren't* you?" Her voice was faint and trembling.

"Adeline, come on."

"First, I taste sour. Now—"

He stopped her with a lingering kiss.

"I love you," he said, "understand? I *love* you. Do you think I'd try to hurt you?"

She shivered in his arms. "You *do* hurt me," she whispered.

He held her close and stroked her hair. He kissed her gently on the lips, the cheeks, the eyes. He told her again and again how much he loved her.

He tried to ignore the smell.

Instantly, his eyes were open and he was listening. He stared up sightlessly into the darkness. Why had he waked up? He turned his head and reached across the mattress. As he touched her, Adeline stirred a little in her sleep.

Norman twisted over on his side and wriggled close to her. He pressed against the yielding warmth of her body, his hand slipping languidly across her hip. He lay his cheek against her back and started drifting downward into sleep again.

Suddenly, his eyes flared open. Aghast, he put his nostrils to her skin and sniffed. An icy barb of dread hooked at his brain; *my God, what's wrong?* He sniffed again, harder. He lay against her, motionless, trying not to panic.

If his senses of taste and smell were atrophying, he could

understand, accept. They weren't, though. Even as he lay there, he could taste the acrid flavor of the coffee that he'd drunk that night. He could smell the faint odor of mashed-out cigarettes in the ashtray on his bedside table. With the least effort, he could smell the wool of the blanket over them.

Then *why?* She was the most important thing in his life. It was torture to him that, in bits and pieces, she was fading from his senses.

It had been a favorite restaurant since their days of courtship. They liked the food, the tranquil atmosphere, the small ensemble which played for dining and for dancing. Searching in his mind, Norman had chosen it as the place where they could best discuss this problem. Already, he was sorry that he had. There was no atmosphere that could relieve the tension he was feeling; and expressing.

"What *else* can it be?" he asked, unhappily. "It's nothing physical." He pushed aside his untouched supper. "It's got to be my mind."

"But why, Norman?"

*"If I only knew,"* he answered.

She put her hand on his. "Please don't worry," she said.

"How can I help it?" he asked. "It's a nightmare. I've *lost* part of you, Adeline."

"Darling, don't" she begged, "I can't bear to see you unhappy."

"I *am* unhappy," he said. He rubbed a finger on the tablecloth. "And I've just about made up my mind to see an analyst." He looked up. "It's got to be my mind," he repeated. "And—damnit!—I resent it. I want to root it out."

He forced a smile, seeing the fear in her eyes.

"Oh, the hell with it," he said. "I'll go to an analyst; he'll fix me up. Come on, let's dance."

She managed to return his smile."

"Lady, you're just plain gorgeous," he told her as they came together on the dance floor.

*"Oh, I love you so,"* she whispered.

It was in the middle of their dance that the feel of her began to change. Norman held her tightly, his cheek forced close to hers so that she wouldn't see the sickened expression on his face.

"And now it's gone?" finished Dr. Bernstrom.

Norman expelled a burst of smoke and jabbed out his cigarette in the ashtray. "Correct," he said, angrily.

"When?"

"This morning," answered Norman. The skin grew taut across his cheeks. "No taste. No smell." He shuddered fitfully. "And now no sense of touch."

His voice broke. "What's wrong?" he pleaded. "What kind of breakdown *is* this?"

"Not an incomprehensible one," said Bernstrom.

Norman looked at him anxiously. "What then?" he asked. "Remember what I said: it has to do only with my wife. Outside of her—"

"I understand," said Bernstrom.

*"Then what is it?"*

"You've heard of hysterical blindness."

"Yes."

"Hysterical deafness."

"Yes, but—"

"Is there any reason, then, there couldn't be an hysterical restraint of the other senses as well?"

"All right, but why?"

Dr. Bernstrom smiled.

"That, I presume," he said, "is why you came to see me."

Sooner or later, the notion had to come. No amount of love could stay it. It came now as he sat alone in the living room, staring at the blur of letters on a newspaper page.

Look at the facts. Last Wednesday night, he'd kissed her and, frowning, said, "You taste sour, honey." She'd tightened, drawn away. At the time, he'd taken her reaction at its obvious value: she felt insulted. Now, he tried to summon up a detailed memory of her behavior afterward.

Because, on Thursday morning, he'd been unable to taste her at all.

Norman glanced guiltily toward the kitchen where Adeline was cleaning up. Except for the sound of her occasional footsteps, the house was silent.

Look at the facts, his mind persisted. He leaned back in the chair and started to review them.

Next, on Saturday, had come that dankly fetid stench. Granted, she should feel resentment if he'd accused her of being its source. But he hadn't; he was sure of it. He'd looked around the kitchen, asked her if she'd put the garbage out. Yet, instantly, she'd assumed that he was talking about her.

And, that night, when he'd waked up, he couldn't smell her.

Norman closed his eyes. His mind must really be in trouble if he could justify such thoughts. He loved Adeline; needed her. How could he allow himself to believe that *she* was, in any way, responsible for what had happened?

Then, in the restaurant, his mind went on, unbidden, while they were dancing, she'd, suddenly, felt cold to him. She'd suddenly, felt—he could not evade the word—*pulpy*.

And, then, this morning—

Norman flung aside the paper. *Stop it!* Trembling, he stared across the room with angry, frightened eyes. It's me, he told himself, *me*! He wasn't going to let his mind destroy the most beautiful thing in his life. He wasn't going to let—

It was as if he'd turned to stone, lips parted, eyes widened, blank. Then, slowly—so slowly that he heard the delicate crackling of bones in his neck—he turned to look toward the kitchen. Adeline was moving around.

Only it wasn't footsteps he heard.

He was barely conscious of his body as he stood. Compelled, he drifted from the living room and across the dining alcove, slippers noiseless on the carpeting. He stopped outside the kitchen door, his face a mask of something like revulsion as he listened to the sounds she made in moving.

Silence then. Bracing himself, he pushed open the door.

Adeline was standing at the opened refrigerator. She turned and smiled.

"I was just about to bring you—" She stopped and looked at him uncertainly. "Norman?" she said.

He couldn't speak. He stood frozen in the doorway, staring at her.

"Norman, what is it?" she asked.

He shivered violently.

Adeline put down the dish of chocolate pudding and hurried toward him. He couldn't help himself; he shrank back with a tremulous cry, his face twisted, stricken.

*"Norman, what's the matter?"*

"I don't know," he whimpered.

Again, she started for him, halting at his cry of terror. Suddenly, her face grew hard as if with angry understanding.

"What is it now?" she asked. "I want to know."

He could only shake his head.

"I want to know, Norman!"

"No." Faintly, frightenedly.

She pressed trembling lips together. "I can't take much more of this," she said. "I mean it, Norman."

He jerked aside as she passed him. Twisting around, he watched her going up the stairs, his expression one of horror as he listened to the noises that she made. Jamming palsied hands across his ears, he stood shivering uncontrollably. *It's me!* he told himself again, again; until the words began to lose their meaning—*me, it's me, it's me, it's me!*

Upstairs, the bedroom door slammed shut. Norman lowered his hands and moved unevenly to the stairs. She had to know that he loved her, that he wanted to believe it was his mind. She had to understand.

Opening the bedroom door, he felt his way through the darkness and sat on the bed. He heard her turn and knew that she was looking at him.

"I'm sorry," he said, "I'm . . . sick."

"No," she said. Her voice was lifeless.

Norman stared at her. "What?"

"There's no problem with other people, our friends,

tradesmen . . ." she said. "They don't see me enough. With you, it's different. We're together too often. The strain of hiding it from you hour after hour, day after day, for a whole year, is too much for me. I've lost the power to control your mind. All I can do is—blank away your senses one by one."

"You're not—"

"—telling you those things are real? I am They're real. The taste, the smell, the—and what you heard tonight."

He sat immobile, staring at the dark form of her.

"I should have taken all your senses when it started," she said, "It would have been easy then. Now it's too late."

"What are you talking about?" He could barely speak.

"It isn't fair." cried her voice. "I've been a good wife to you! Why should I have to go back? I *won't* go back! I'll find somebody else. I won't make the same mistake next time!"

Norman jerked away from her and stood on wavering legs, his fingers clutching for the lamp.

*"Don't touch it!"* ordered the voice.

The light flared blindingly into his eyes. He heard a thrashing on the bed and whirled. He couldn't even scream. Sound coagulated in his throat as he watched the shapeless mass rear upward, dripping decay.

"All right!" the words exploded in his brain with the illusion of sound. "All right, then *know* me!"

All his senses flooded back at once. The air was clotted with the smell of her. Norman recoiled, lost balance, fell. He saw the moldering dead bulk rise from the bed and start for him. Then his mind was swallowed in consuming blackness and it seemed as if he fled along a night-swept hall pursued by a suppliant voice which kept repeating endlessly, "Please! I don't want to go back! *None of us want to go back!* Love me, let me stay with you! love me, love me, love me . . ."

# Miss Stardust

Dear Harry:

How are things in the baked bean industry? Cracky good, I trust—as we used to say in those halcyon days of yore when thou and mou were dripping young ichor over our public relations courses at ye olde M.U.

I swan things *should* be cracky good, what with your future intact and paid-for Cadillac. Second-rank publicity man for Altshuler's Boston Beauties. Kid, you're living.

As for me—nothing. I'm on the ropes from this dang Miss Stardust contest. I s'pose you've read some accounts of the debacle by our comrades-in-legs, the roving reporters. Well, buddy, the inside tale is still to be wagged. So I'm waggin'. List.

To begin with, as they prose in Victorian ghost stories, I have my little agency, single, entrepreneurish and struggling. I have no complaints. There are my steady customers—Garshbuller's Candied Dental Floss, Los Alamos Insect Bombs, The Blue Underwear Company, and, but of course, the ever popular Mae Bushkins Imperial Foundations. All said clients guaranteed to knock me out a steady if nonstratospheric return.

So what happens? You remember that joker from my home town I told you about once, Gad Simpkins? You know, the one who was going to parachute down a mine shaft? The one who was going to walk tightrope across a burning Bessemer converter? Sure you do.

What happens but the jerk decides to swim the English Channel backstroke. Damn fool thing to try in any man's book, but that was Gad to the socks. Always one for a new twist.

Well, to cut short the prelims, Gad doesn't know a soul. He's small potatoes, strictly a benchwarmer in the minor leagues. He comes to me. Joe, he says, you got to handle my publicity for the swim. This is dynamite, he says to me. I look him over. Change your brand, I tell him. He retires.

But comes two plot thickeners. For one, Los Alamos Insect Bombs is kaput, after one of its larger items blows up a customer's seven-room house and adjoining garage, while he and family are out to the movies.

Result: A—One less client. B—Enough loss to create one wry look on the kisser of my beloved, which says as clearly as if she'd intoned the words in her gravelly snarl: *''Penury. It's upon us!''*

This is the first thing. The second is edging on the subtler side, but still enough to egg me on. I am getting sick of dental floss and foundations and blue underwear. I am tired of catering to torsos and teeth. I want a little magic in my latter days. Besides the fact, as I say, that I covet a little needed jack to improve my low-caste status at Home Sweet Home.

But enough of that. Sufficient to say that I give the job a run for its money. All the tricks of the trade, from squibs to bits of semi-droll fluff in *The New Yorker* magazine. I get Gad on the radio, he desports like the idiot he is. You know the rest. Good solid publicity, interest snowballing, project going strong. Is it my fault Gadstone Simpkins swims into a rock twenty yards out from the Gallic shoreline?

So I toss my graying shock of hair to the side, and am preparing my retreat to blue underwear, when to the house comes a party of three. They are directors of a proposed contest to determine who is to be a certain Miss Stardust.

I elucidate, this being the crux of my somber plaint. The winner of this here contest is to be declared best-looking head not only on Earth, not only in the Solar System, but in the whole blarsted galaxy. This includes *beaucoup* stars and this, my skinny info about the heavens informs me, includes the chance of a goodly sum of probable life-sustaining planets. As well as our own nine, one of which we already know contains a strange brand of living matter.

Ergo—mishmosh.

However, at the moment these three talent-seeking gents come to see me, I am not thinking overhard about such wraithlike topics. I know as much astronomy as I know where last year's taxes went. When it comes to supernova and escape velocities, I am on a par with the guy who can lose a bass drum in a telephone booth.

This, I hasten to add, disturbs me not one whit. Because the three characters like my publicity work on Gad's ill-fated swim. I have imagination. I have the fresh approach. I have journalistic *joie de vivre*. Outcome—they want me to handle the Miss Stardust contest at a juicy figure (not one of their prospective contestants—a retainer).

I sign the contract. Hastily. I am now head rah-rah man for a setup that determines which babe has the face that launches a thousand spaceships.

So I get hep. I start ladling out the pabulum of publicity articles and ads disguised as news. 8 × 10 glossies make the rounds. Miss Georgia and Miss New York and Miss Transylvania and Miss Hemoglobin and Miss The Girl We'd Most Like To Be Trapped in a Cement Mixer With.

Prizes are announced. A huge silver loving cup. A Hollywood contract. A car. Others. The applications pour in.

Interest picks up. The boardwalk at Long Harbor starts to get prettied up. The judges are picked, five of them. Two are local dignitaries, fugitives from the Chamber of Commerce. One is a Mayor Grassblood on his yearly vacation from Gall Stone, Arizona. Another is Marvin O'Shea, president of a chemical plant. Last and least is Gloober, of Gloober and Gloober, old firm of good repute that turns out bathing suits. (Guess what kind of bathing suits all contestants are going to wear.)

Everything is going cracky good. Excitement fills the air. Drivel fills the columns. Merchants are rubbing their gnarled palms together, oiling up the wheels on their cash register drawers. Middle-aged men are packing duds and combing out toupees to attend the festival. Joy to the world. Everyone is animate. Especially me. I am raking in such matchless coin that I am tempted to slip Mae Bushkin the word to take a flying leap into blue underwear while drawing candied dental floss between the gaps in her bridge. But caution prevails. My wife's middle name. She says you never can tell.

Truer words were never growled.

Because what happens, but three days before the contest starts Mrs. Local Dignitary Number One gets a severe case of galloping undefinable, and ends up in the hospital. Old Man Local Dignitary Number One gets the shakes, cancels his job, and hies to the bedside with roses and condolences. A solid marital gesture, but rough on the contest.

We replace him with Sam Sampson, who owns five car lots. This is not too bad, because we now sidestep the need to hire cars for the babes to ride around Long Harbor in, and cause all male viewers to wax pop-eyed viewing how little material old man Gloober weaves into his bathing suits.

So we are all squared off again. Until Marvin O'Shea, president of a chemical plant, is driving to see an infirm aunt in La Jolla, when his right rear goes "pow," and he and his ever-nagging go ploughing through the last two cabins of Mackintoshe's Little Hawaiian Motel.

The duo is not seriously injured, but both end up in the white place, flat on their backs and sniffing flowers of compassion. That takes care of another judge.

With mutters of "jinx" in our ears we find ourselves yet another replacement. Said replacement promptly gets himself in a drunken street brawl, and we have to ease him out of the picture fast. He screams foul and, true, it does seem undue odd. The joker has laid off the bottle for twenty-seven years. But testimony prevails. It emerges clear that the old gent had enough alcohol in him to light seventeen hurricane lamps.

We make the bid to replace this unfortunate with one Saul Mendelheimer, owner and producer of Mendelheimer's Garden-of-Eden Pickles. Mandelheimer acquiesces. We are set again. The machine shudders on.

Then, the day before the contest is to start, the pier collapses. Luckily no one is on it but Lewisohn Tamarkis, who is arranging floral wreaths. He dog-paddles to shore, whilst cursing all living things, and drives off, dripping Pacific Ocean on the seat covers of his 1948 Studebaker.

Our brows knit with grave suspicions. Mutters of "Communists" falling from many a furtive lip, we acquire the Municipal Auditorium. This is not so good as the outdoors, but our hands are tied. I for one, being a superstitious crank, think there is a curse operating on the show. I have dealt with such ill-fated projects in my time and, say I, once a deal starts going sour there's nothing you can do.

This Miss Stardust contest was accursed, I decided. I didn't know the half of it.

So where was I? Oh, yeah. Well, we finally manage to reach the morning of the show with five breathing, walking judges. The day dawns bright and rainy. First time it rains on that date since 1867. We're all burned. The judges sit in their hotel suite and grouse. Get to the auditorium, I tell them. Then I run around trying to get things rolling.

First I send out sixteen Sampson cars with loudspeakers, and Long Harbor is informed that The Show Will Go On. On top to each car is a broad, gamuting from Miss Alsace-Lorraine to Miss Pitkin Avenue. They are dressed in flesh-colored bathing suits and transparent raincoats. They hold umbrellas with one hand and wave with the other. They giggle and give the come-on over the mike. If this, plus flesh-colored suits, fails, I will concede all to be over, and will wire Mae Bushkin for a rematch.

Also I send out little boys with handbills. I snatch a few minutes of radio time and get a local happyvoice announcer to give out with a come one, come all. I send up a balloon. *See Miss Stardust Today!!* it says. Someone shoots it down. A prankster, I think.

Not so.

After a morning of hasty relations with the public, I hie to the auditorium for a last confab with the judges. I note that carpenters are still banging away on the judges' booth on stage. A dry Lewisohn Tamarkis and crew are heaving bouquets around. I think we may get this show on the road yet.

Then it comes.

I step into the elevator and zip up the shaft. I patter down the hallway. I enter the judges' room.

"Men," I say.

And that's all.

Because they are sitting paralyzed in their chairs, gaping at a thing in the middle of the floor to which my eyes move.

My lower jaw hits the laces of my Florsheims.

Ever see a vacuum cleaner? With a head of cabbage on top? With a jacket on? Standing in the middle of a rug and giving you the eye?

Kiddo, I did.

I am verging on swoon when it addresses me.

"You are in charge?" it inquires.

I do not reply. My tongue is tied. It is strapped. My eyes roll out and bounce on the floor. Nearly.

The thing looks piqued—as much as a head of cabbage can look piqued.

"Very well," he-she-it says, "since no one present seems capable of speech, I shall state our case and depart."

*Our* case. I feel my skin tightening. We are all riven to our spots. We listen to the mechanical voice of the thing. No mouth is to be seen. Its pronunciation is stilted. It is something like hearing a monologue from that train that says "*Bromo Seltzer, Bromo Seltzer, Bromo Seltzer.*"

"This contest," it says, "is declared void."

Then, as he looks us over with his one oval eye, I get me a glimmer. In my long years as drudge, rabblerouser and savant of the public taste, I have seen many a weirdie in operation.

So I watch this article with sage eyes. I ponder the angle.

"I will elucidate," says cabbage head, "should your silence indicate vacuity of perception. You have, most inappropriately named this tourney the Miss Stardust contest. Since your microbic Earth, as you call it, represents no more than the most infinitesimal mote in this galaxy, your choice of contest titling is more than inexpedient. It has been considered noxiously naive and insulting to a serious degree.''

*Too* clever, I thought, too all-fire verbose. Nobody spiels like so except the English Department at Cambridge. This is a frame, I deduce. Someone is kidding us.

Used to know a guy named Campbell Gault. He made those novelties like joy buzzers and fake spiders and ashtrays that look like outhouses. Old Camp used to make robots, too. Once during the war he had a steel Hirohito clanking up old 42nd Street singing *I'm a Japanese Sandman*. Clever, and just the sort of john to play a gag like this.

''Is this understood?'' says the cabbage skull with a toss of his leaves.

I smile knowingly. I look at the transfixed judges.

''All right,'' I say, ''let's cut it. We have work to do.''

''Sit down,'' says the thing. ''I am not addressing you.''

''Go find yourself some corned beef,'' I say.

''I warn you.''

''Bromo Seltzer, Bromo Seltzer,'' I reply.

I find myself pinned to the broadloom by a bluish ray that buzzes out from the vacuum cleaner. It feels something like when you stand on one of those penny Foot Easers. Lots of vibration, and a numbing sensation. But I'm not standing on anything. I'm flat on my back.

''Hey!'' I yell, confounded.

''May that strike some reason into you,'' quoth the vacuum cleaner. ''I will now conclude my statement.''

The thing rolls around the floor, concluding.

''As I was saying before this intemperate intrusion on my words,'' he says, ''since your molecular planet is but the minutest portion of the vast spaces which this contest presumes to encompass, we can only assume grave intolerance, and demand retraction.''

''May I . . .'' commences Mendelheimer of Mendelheimer's Garden-of-Eden Pickles, 'May I, ulp, inquire . . . w-w-where you are from?''

''I have just arrived from Asturi Cridenta, as you might call it in your primitive linguistics.''

"A...a...a..." Mendelheimer gags.

"An extraterrestrial!" gasps Sam Sampson, who reads science fiction, between hooking car lovers.

"W-what do you want?"

That's me, a faint squeak in the vicinity of the carpet.

"One of two things," replies the interplanetary vegetable. "A change in the contest title, or representation."

"But..." from me.

"I will remind you," said the appliance from outer space, "we have the necessary potency to apply coercion on this body."

"Co-*ercion*?" says Gloober of Gloober and etcetera.

"We have already attempted to disappoint furtherance of this affair," says you-know-what, "but to no apparent avail."

"The accidents," murmur I.

"The pier!" cries Mendelheimer.

"The fight!" Sampson snaps words and fingers.

"The rain," says the vacuum cleaner.

"I *knew* it!" ejaculates Local Dignitary Number Two. "It never rains in Long Harbor unless there is foul play!"

"This is beside the actual point," says our visitor. "Being now aware of our potential effect, judge accordingly."

Outside, rain is dribbling on the windows. Inside, Judges are dribbling on their cravats. I am pale, and fain would conk out. We look at the cabbage, which poses a truculent pose on the rug.

"How d-did you get in here?" asks Mendelheimer.

"Make your decision," states the thing. "You will have the contest title changed, or accord us due representation."

"But, look," I start in, forgetting momentarily my head-to-toe hotfoot.

His eye is on me. I subside.

"We are not here to haggle." The Bromo Seltzer train rattles angrily over a trestle. "The decision is made. Do not strain our patience."

Public relations to the rescue.

"But, look," I proceed. "We've already got a thousand

posters that read *Miss Stardust Contest*. We've advertised that name. We've sold advance-ticket blocks and the tickets read *Admit One to the Miss Stardust Contest*. Concessionaires have balloons that read..."

"Balloons can be punctured," says cabbage head, yet testier.

"You did that," I murmur, "*too*?"

"Enough of this!" bristles the vacuum cleaner from the black velocities. "If you wish to retain your title, then we demand representative rights."

In my true hack mind, Harry, already are wheels turning and buzzers buzzing and little factory workers hustling. The potential spread is before my mental eyes.

> SEE MISS STARDUST!! THE BEAUTY OF THE HEAVENS!!! PULCHRITUDE FROM BEYOND THE STARS!!!! THE GREATEST, THE MOST SENSATIONAL!!!!

Exclamation point.

"All right," I say, getting the jump on a stunned board of judges, "you've got it."

"Now, *one* moment please." The mayor of Gall Stone, Arizona, starts a slow-fission bombast. "This calls for discussion."

"Discussion!" I say, still flat on my back. "What do you want them to do—disintegrate the Municipal Auditorium?"

Local Dignitary Number Two leaps to his brogans.

"No sir!" he cries. "Not the Municipal Auditorium!"

Silence upon the babbling. The vacuum cleaner gives us the once-over heavily.

"Make your decision," he warns.

So we all nod, pale at the gills.

"Very well," he says.

"How long will it take to get your entry here?" I inquire politely.

"I will inform the member units of the alliance," he tells us. "The entries will be here within the hour."

"Entry-zzzz?" I gurgle.

"There are several thousand," he says.

I sag back on the carpeting. I appraise the ceiling and wish I am back plugging the virtues of blue underwear. I envision a stage sagging with several thousand interplanetary broads. I cannot envision the sight of female vacuum cleaners in Gloober bathing suits.

"Thousands?" gulps Mendelheimer.

"I note reluctance," says cabbage skull. "Your alternative is the simple act of changing the contest title."

"We're ruined," says Gloober.

The yellow eye softens.

"As a matter of actual point," he says, "I named such a high figure in hopes of forcing you to accept the alternative. However, I see that you cannot. Know then that beyond your own system, our alliance has determined its own Miss Stardust, though hardly," he added snottily, "by that title. We will consent to allow her to represent the remainder of this galaxy. She, plus the four contestants from your own system, will make five. Fairness beyond this you cannot expect to receive."

"Four...in our system?" Sampson asks.

"There is no movable life on the four outermost planets of your system."

Now I am no devotee of Astronomy, Harry, but even for me, this is a hell of a way to get the word about life on other worlds. From the lips of an abusive cabbage. Lips? What lips?

Well, to make a grotesque story short, we accept the conditions. We pick up his under-the-deck deal. If the talking Hoover can make piers collapse and skies liquify, who are we to argue with him? We say, "You win," and everything is cracky bad.

After that the vacuum cleaner from another world exits. Exeunt all on his heels, to view him passing through the hall ceiling, head first. We discover later, from a gibbering roof janitor, that cabbage head bazookas himself up through the skylight and floats up to his interstellar crockery, which is hovering fifty feet over the building. Said saucer then whips into the blue yonder and is gone. As is the composure of one formerly sane janitor.

The judges and I have a session. A couple of them get brave and cry fraud. I tell them off. I inform them that they are not pinned to the floor by blue light and I am. They reflect on this.

The upshot is we have cards painted for the contestants we expect. I do the painting, not wishing to let some hand-painter blab about the new cards he did. I consult Sampson for the information. There should be a card for Miss Mercury, he says, one for Miss Venus, two others for Miss Mars and Miss Jupiter. Of course, he says, they doubtless have different names for their planets. Not withstanding, blusters Mayor Grassblood, if they are taking part in an Earth contest, they'll take our names for them or leave them. I remind him of cabbage head making the rain, collapsing the pier and playing elevator with himself through the floors. Grassblood pauses a moment to reflect on that.

We deduce a slight problem on the title card for the last contestant. We cannot call her Miss Stardust because, by the standards of the contest, she ain't yet. But the vacuum cleaner says she is *Their* Miss Stardust. So what to do? We settle for an unsatisfactory Miss Outer Space.

"The monster will not take a shine to that," forbodes Mendelheimer.

We hush him up. We retire to the elevator, punchy but unbowed, wondering what the day will bring.

It brings headaches.

We decide to spread none of this about since we're not sure. I don't mean we're not sure the vacuum cleaner doesn't mean business, we're not sure we should let cat from bag, lest the walls of the auditorium get kicked down by the eager.

But, as per usual, some creep on the inside gives out with a strictly-between-you-and-me, and before you can say Coma Berenices the place is crawling with rumor. Add the eyewitness of one hysterical frump who sights the crockery take off over the auditorium, and you have the seeds, the ripe beginning, and the rotten harvest.

I am stopped. Is it true about the saucer, they ask, about the literate head of cabbage? Ha ha, I say, that's a good one.

Reaching the stage forty minutes and many ha ha's later, I find out how good a one it really is.

The contestants have shown with their delegate, coach and chaperone, cabbage head. All the babes who are stacked in Earthly manner are gaping like kids at a sideshow. They stand around in their Gloober suits with their eyes popping out.

This the delegate does not like. Because, when I extend my hand with a Kingfish smile, the big yellow eye flashes over me like the headlight on a locomotive. I see there is nothing to shake anyway, swallow a faux pas lump, and pretend not to notice.

"Well, you made it," I chirp.

"Did you doubt it?" says he in a surly gasp which has all the amiablity of a Bendix washer conversing.

"No! No!" I say, jollity flecking off my ashen jowls. "Not at all. We've been waiting for you."

He ignores that. He gives the people on stage the single eye. He hisses.

"My wards are losing patience with your goggling Earthians. I demand you have the contest started immediately and see to it that this offensive staring ceases."

I nod, I smile, I make the rounds dispersing, my stomach doing pushups. That completed, I return to the vacuum cleaner. He says something which makes my heart bounce like a handball.

"If," he says, "I note the slightest prejudice toward my wards, the remotest suggestion of alien regard—there will be severe repercussions."

And so drags on stage the contest née Miss Stardust.

Ever have a dream where everything goes wrong? Where no matter what you try, it backfires? Where you're the eternal blunderer? That's what I feel like in that contest. The thing is a shambles.

There is a long rumble of curiosity when, after a few Earth

babes have minced on and off stage, we hold up the card that reads *Miss Mercury*. Then a few hoots and cat-calls. These suddenly ending when the kid herself makes her entrance.

Now if a technicolor rock comes bobbing out on a stage, Harry, what would you do? The same as the audience did, I speck. Eyeballs protrude, faces blank, jaws gape; in a thousand brains comes the sole query:

Wot in 'ell is this?

Then some visiting fireman gives out with a guffaw and that starts it off. They all decide this is a wonderful gag. I glance a queasy shot over my trembling shoulder and see murder in that yellow eye. My Adam's apple does a swan dive into my lungs, and I turn back.

Applause now. Great little gag that, ha ha. Bring on some more. Some more comes.

Miss Venus.

A hothouse plant with eyes. It slips across the stage on its bottom fronds. The eyes, three, look around the audience. They look ever so slightly disgusted.

Another roar from the audience, this one a little forced. Like the roar of a man who, by gosh, is going to have a good time even if his hair *is* starting to stand on end. This gag is almost *too* good. A guy could swear that green plant was walking around by itself, the wires are so well concealed.

I smell a breath over my shoulder. Rather foul.

"This reception is highly unsatisfactory," bubbles cabbage head. "You will alleviate the situation or there will be increasing trouble for you."

I look at him. I think of flying saucers and ray guns and California going up in toto.

That in mind, I bounce out on stage as Miss Venus exits. I raise the mike from the floor. I raise my palsied arms.

"May I have your attention," my voice booms through the place. Only electrically.

Brief pause in pandemonium.

"Listen, people," I say, "I know this is hard to swallow but those two contestants you just saw are really from Mercury and..."

I am laughed to scorn. I am inundated by Bronx cheers. A cushion flies in the air. Mocking airplanes fashioned from programs fill the auditorium sky. Confetti drizzles from the balconies.

"Wait a minute!" I shout. "Your attention please."

More noise. I wait for the subsiding. I see flashbulb lightning everywhere. Story and pix will be in the newspapers posthaste. For the first time, unworked-for publicity gives me a pain. Let's face it, I'm scared, Harry. When heroes were made, I was sleeping one off in the next room.

"Let's be fair to these contestants," I say, my voice a lustrous croak. "Let's show them some real Earthlike sportsmanship."

I then let loose a flimsy wave of hand, sheathe the mike in the floor, beckon to the m.c. to take over, and traipse off stage. Right into the vacuum cleaner. I raise a shaky smile to the edifice of his dubious good nature. He glares at me.

"Miss Mercury is grossly offended," he tells me. "She states that if she is not chosen winner of the contest, there will be severe retaliation by her elders."

*"What!"*

I recoil against the curtain.

"Now wait a second," I gasp. "Have a heart. We can't rig the contest just because . . ."

I'm talking to deaf ears. To no ears, to be correct.

"You created your own problem," he says, "when you named your contest as you did."

"Buddy, *I* didn't name it!"

"Beside the actual point," he says, and wheels off. I turn back to the stage with haunted blinkers. Just in time to get a fast load of Miss Mars making her debut on old Earth.

More like an hors d'oeuvre than a female. The trunk and head are two Spanish olives, and the legs and arms are toothpicks stuck in them. I hang onto the curtain ropes with a sorry groan. The audience isn't catcalling so much now. It is sinking in. Even though it's a hard thing to admit and still claim sanity. You see a couple of olives stroll on stage, preceded by an ambulating tropical plant and a rainbow rock that crawls and first you laugh it off, then the creeps get to you.

The creeps are getting to them.

Miss Jupiter doesn't help any when she slides across stage in a transparent globe. She looks like a dirty iceberg. No face, arms legs—no nothing. I hear someone in the audience gag. Someone says ugh. All we need now, I am thinking is...

"Miss Mars has informed me," the vacuum cleaner says, "that unless she wins first prize, her injured emotions will result in venomous impulses toward revenge against this planet."

"Now, *wait* a minute, buddy," I implore.

"Finish the contest quickly," he says. "My wards are becoming violently ill at the sight of Earth people en masse."

"What do you mean, ill?"

"They find your appearance surpassingly repugnant," he says.

"Now, *look*," I say.

He is gone.

I watch him roll off. They find *us* repugnant. If I were not ready to cry I would laugh. But I am ready to cry.

Highlight of the show, Miss Stardust, their own Miss Stardust, comes out of the wings.

I can't say she walked. She didn't roll. It wasn't a crawl. You might say she slobbered her way across the stage.

She was an orange jellyfish with a skirt and eyes. She was some jello quivering from the bowl in search of whipped cream. I better shut up, I'm making myself sick.

No, I keep telling myself, *she* wouldn't do that. She couldn't possibly think that...

"Our Miss Stardust has informed me..." starts the delegate.

That's all, brother.

"Oh she has!" I yell. "What's the matter with Venus and Jupiter, are they sick?"

"They also demand first prize," says the vacuum cleaner with the head like a cabbage.

I melt, I drip into the floorboards and disappear between the cracks. In wishful imagination anyway. I really just stand there, my mouth offering a large home for needy flies.

"How can they *all* win?" I ask in a gurgling mutter.

"Beside the actual point," *he* says and *I* think in unison.

Briefly, my dander goes up again.

"I think you came here just to start trouble," I tell him.

His eye is on me like an exterminator's lining sights on a particularly odious specimen.

"We do not like you Earthmen," he says. "My wards and I find you both obnoxious to the mind and unwholesome to the eye. My wards and I will be glad when they have all won first prize and can leave your loathsome presence."

I stare at his receding dustbag back. I ponder slipping out the back way and hopping a raft for South America. In the pit the band is playing "I'm in Love with the Man in the Moon," the only interplanetary song they know. The judges are stumbling off stage for a break, looking for a good ten fingers of anything potent. They had become judges in the hope of rousing senile corpuscles by viewing luscious femalia. Instead . . . this.

I shepherd them all into a dressing room the size of an occupied closet. They all stand there with untended sweat drops dripping from their portly faces. They direct smitten eyes in my direction.

"We have a first-class hellish problem," I tell them. I enlarge.

"But . . . *that's impossible*!" cries Local Dignitary Number Two, unable to smite his noble brow because the room is too small.

"I've told him that," I say. "He's not buying."

Gloober of etcetera and etcetera sinks down into a chair which just manages to support ample him.

"I'm sick," he announces.

Grassblood pounds his well-pounded palm.

"This is un-American!" he says and purses lips.

"And I have a niece who wanted to win the contest," says Mendelheimer sadly.

"What!" cries Local Dig 2. "Fraud! Calumny!"

"Awright awready—*stow it*!" That is an angry me, fed up to here.

I ease immediate tension. I tell Mendelheimer that even if his niece, Miss Alimentary Canal, is impartially judged best-looking head, she can't win now because we are hung up. One of the outer spacers *has* to get the prize.

"Or. . .*what*?" asks Gloober of.

"Or else we get pulverized," I say.

"You think they can really do this thing?" asks Mendelheimer.

"Buddy, after what I've seen that character do, I'll take his word on the rest."

"But which contestant should we give it to?" Sampson poses the big question.

Local Dig 2 throws up his hands in municipal despair.

"We are trapped!" he cries.

I think so too.

Well, we have to adjourn, because the contest must go on. I advise them to stall as long as possible, measure everything twice, ogle slow. They file back to their stand with the gaiety of nobles climbing into tumbrils. They sit there, and I know they are worried when Miss Brooklyn writhes by and they don't bat an eyelash. When such a stack passing before the eye causes no reaction, you are either powerful worried or you are dead.

Again I attempt to reason with cabbage head.

"Look," I say, "you're intelligent. Isn't it obvious that we can't give *one* prize to *five* contestants?"

Earthian math is lost on him.

"This contest must end soon," is all he tells me. "This superficial chatter is merely irritating us further. There is obviously no competition between my lovely wards and those hideous creatures parading out there. No judge, be he of Earth or Heaven, could possibly award a prize to such manifest hideousness."

Glimmers. A germ.

"*Hideous*?" I say. "You think they're hideous?"

"You are *all* hideous."

I turn away. Suddenly I have it. My brain is clicking at last. I rush to a phone and make my bid to save poor Earth.

Then I ease on stage and slide in beside Sampson. There, while eyeing morsels of perfect 36-22-36, I slip him the word from the corner of my mouth.

He breaks into the smile reserved for cash buyers of this year's Cadillac. Then he leans over and whispers the news to Gall Stone's civic pride. The mayor passes it on to Mendelheimer's shell-like ears, Mendelheimer to Gloober and Gloober to Loc Dig 2.

Now they are all grinning and looking with revitalized leers at passing pulchritude, and I am feeling like a very clever publicity man.

This is probably the longest beauty contest known to man. It has to be. My plan needs time, and we have to buy it expensive. We have the contestants coming on frontways, sideways and backwards. Singly, in pairs, in groups, and in a long zoftic line. They do everything but walk on their hands. The babes start jawing about it. Even the audience gets a gutful of willowy shapes. And when glassy-eyed males get tired of looking at babes, man, you've overdone it.

But by then it is all right, because my plan is ready to go.

I go to the mike.

"Ladies and gentlemen," I say. "Before we announce our winner, I want to add another surprise award to our list of prizes. We had formerly announced the loving cup, the car, the Hollywood contract, the year's free servicing and chassis work at Max Factor's, and other smaller items. Now we have another prize."

I pause for my coup.

"A month's vacation in the Mediterranean with none other than . . ."

I wave my arm toward the wings.

"Ladies and gentlemen," I ham it, "*Mister Universe!*"

The big blond giant comes padding out in his tights, and fed-up housewives do nip-ups in their seats.

While the cheers and groans ring out over my weary but

joyous head, I gaze off stage.

As I figure, the broads from space are crowding around their delegate. I nod to the m.c. and amble off the boards, my mind cool with victory.

So we're hideous, are we? Well, that's too bad. If they want the first prize, they have to take that vacation too. A month in the Mediterranean with Mister Manifest Hideousness. Take it or leave it.

Cabbage head spies me now, and whizzes across the floor. I gulp as he approaches, the feeling of victory sort of dying. That eye looks *mad.*

"You attempt trickery!" he accuses me.

"Trickery?" I make with the bland face.

"You intend to carry this ruse out?" he asks.

"Mister," I say, "this is *our* contest. We'll give you first prize, but we have the right to say what the prize will be."

"Beside the actual point," he says.

"*What*?" I feel something giving.

"How *dare* you proclaim that creature Mister Universe!" he gargles. "Are you not aware that the Universe contains more galaxies than there are stars in your *own* galaxy?

"Huh?"

"This calls for drastic action. I must call immediately on the alliance of galaxies. There will be a contest held in this building to decide who is really entitled to the name Mister Universe. Let me see, there are approximately seven million, five hundred and ninety-five thousand base representatives which, divided into their integral parts, makes . . ."

Harry, what do you say? Can you use a weak assistant to help you push beans? Harry I'll work for nothing. Please!

JOE

# Full Circle

The city editor called him in. "Here," he said. He tossed a ticket across his desk. "For tonight."

Walt picked up the ticket. "Are you kidding?" he asked.

Barton rested his head on his hands. He looked mildly quizzical. He said, "Thompson, do I strike you as the kidding sort?"

Walt grinned. "Yeah," he said, "like Macbeth."

He started out. At the door, he turned. "How shall it be?" he asked. "Straight? Humorous? Allegorical? Historical-pastoral? Scene undivided or poem unlimited?"

"You may get the hell out of here," Barton said.

As he moved through the press room, Walt looked at the ticket again. *January 25, 2231. Terwilliger's Living Marionettes,* it announced. *Larg and Fellow Martians in "Rip Van Winkle."*

"Oh me, oh my," cried his wife, "we will starve to death. You are a lazy good-for-nothing, you Rip Van Winkle!"

I sat lost in a heaving lava bed of children.

Their eyes were like abacus beads sliding. They couldn't sit still. They plucked at clothes and nose. They sucked and gobbled on candy bars. They whispered, they giggled, they threw paper rocket ships at each other.

Incidentally, they watched Terwilliger's Living Marionettes.

"You go and you find some work!" howled Mrs. Rip Van Winkle.

It drew an appreciative chuckle from oldsters at conditions

before Position Bureau assured one hundred per cent employment. Mrs. R. Van W. tearing at his mop-hued wig—Martians are bald as we know.

"You get out of this house and get a job!"

"Yah, yah!" replied Rip in a breathless squeak. "Yah, yah, I go."

He sticks a floppy hat on his large skull. His head swells outsize to his body. It makes him look like a caricature.

He is bent over and skinny. He is all angular joints and spaghetti extremities. He is dressed in old patched clothes hanging like robes on a skeleton. He is two feet tall.

"Yah, yah," he says, repeating the line because kiddies guffaw when he says it. Guffaws drift to plucking, eating, shifting, picking, throwing, whispering, shouting.

Rip gets his gun. It falls apart. There are gales of appreciation. The auditorium is dark except for the stage.

The scene is an old Dutch kitchen, says the program. Preindustrial period. Around 1750, to judge from the set. That's a long time ago. A pretty good story to last six centuries. But does it last so we may enjoy—or perhaps so we may scoff?

She is chasing him out of the kitchen with a broom, an obsolete cleaning utensil. Straw, bound together for purpose of collecting dirt and trash in a contiguous pile. Kiddies don't know that. They think it's something for hitting.

"You get out of here, you lazy good-for-nothing!" she howls.

She hits him over the head. Once. Twice. *Bang, bang!* Kiddies roar, tug at their clothes, their neighbors' clothes, clap their pudgy pink hands, show their white teeth in savage pleasure.

Savage? Dear reader, do you raise eyebrows at that word applied to your children? Do you put down your paper, purse indignant lips? Do you ask yourself in silent outrage—who is this jackanapes, this critic, this vile assaulter on the high-blown walls of parenthood?

You do? But read on.

Out goes Rip! Flying through the double door. *Flop!* Into

the dust of the road. Mrs. R. Van W. boots the dog, Wolf, after its master. The dog is only a doll made up as a dog. The Martians are too small. A real dog would fill the stage. A real dog might eat the actors.

"And don't come back without a job!" she cries out, fierce and indignant.

She plops in a chair. Her wig slips over her face. Pandemonium. The curtain dances out and meets itself. It shudders to a draping halt.

In the return to self I think of how almost shocking it was to see that wig come sliding off.

Like dignity fluttering down to fall beneath trampling feet.

Intermission.

The play forgotten, the kiddies crowded into the aisles. Time to stuff in more candy and soda and ice cream and cake and fighting. More rocket ships arched in graceful swoops through the theater air.

I remained in my seat, listening to the raging storm of children together. Watching the maelstrom of activity that is the mark of youth. I picked the ticket stub from my coat pocket.

*Terwilliger's Living Marionettes.*

A minor note of prescience tugged at my mind. The words were contradictory I realized suddenly—apparently for the first time.

Marionettes are not living.

And I sat thinking—of the little man and his ragged clothes, of the shrill-voiced woman, hitting and shrieking.

And then I realized that the children were howling at living things. And something tightened in me.

And stayed tight.

Second act.

The mass of children was somehow shoehorned back in place. The auditorium was like an overstuffed trunk, its edges bulging. Bits of children popped up from the pressure of excitement.

The curtain opened. A flitting moment of hush. Then another scene.

Rip and his flat-faced dog trudged into a country glade. Dandruff-crowned mountains from the background, undulating slightly as breezes move the backdrop. *The power to move mountains,* the phrase occurs to me.

"Oh me, oh my, I'm so tired," says Rip.

He flops down and his feet go in the air. No one notices the look of pain that flares up in his narrow face—no one except me. I look at him carefully as he goes on mouthing childish words. This is Larg, the star. And are those lines in his face from makeup or from misery?

He leans against a fake tree trunk and looks around.

*Brroom! Brroom!*

"Oh my, what is that?" he asks his dog.

His dog says "Woof!" Without its face changing an iota. "*Woof!*" again. Its voice drops down from the sky. It is noticeable because it is the only real marionette in this marionette show.

*Brroom!*

Up jumps Rip. He says, "I will look and see what it is!"

He starts off, pretending to walk while the backdrop creaks along on rollers and the tree is tugged offstage by dreadfully visible wires.

I watched him.

I forgot the show. The Martian was limping. There were lines of anguish in his face, obviously not etched with makeup pencils.

He was in pain. But no one noticed it. Not the parents, not the children. Who looks for pain in a piece of wood.

But perhaps I bestow a sensitivity on myself which was not present at that moment.

For it is later now, you see, and as I sit here writing of it, I have it *all*. Not just disconcerting fragments born in the midst of seething children.

Why tell more of the show? It's not important. The little men, perhaps six inches tall, bowling marbles while someone is back shook a sheet of tin and made theatrical thunder. That's not important.

The giving to Rip of drink from a minute barrel. Rip choking and coughing, lying down to sleep. And the curtain closing and the lights staying out. And the children rustling like swishing grasses in the blackness.

All unimportant.

And the rest of it too. The curtain opening on Rip, still there, long white whiskers on his face. Rip getting up.

Perhaps it *is* important that Larg looked more natural as a tired old man than he had before. But the rest is of no moment.

And as I sat there, paying scant attention, I decided to go backstage and talk to Larg if I could. It would be better, I thought, than just handing in an ordinary review. Barton liked ingenuity.

But that was a pretext. There was more—more than just a Rip Van Winkle and a twenty-year sleep and an afternoon's entertainment for a mob of pink-chopped children.

And so it ended. Rip back in town, his wife dead, the old political regime unseated, Rip almost shot as a spy. And the happy ending, as per requirement, with Rip sitting under a tree, children about him. Happy days are here again. Curtain.

One call for the actors. They stood stiffly, nodding their heads. Their eyes glittered from the footlights. And it was a sick glitter, the glitter in their eyes.

I went backstage. The little Martians were rushing around, carrying costumes, equipment, scenery. They didn't look at me. They ran past my legs. Their heads just reached my kneecaps. It was like a dream. You don't see Martians en masse very often. It was like being Gulliver all of a sudden.

I saw a man sitting on a stool, leaning against the wall as he read a paper. Every once in a while he'd lift his eyes to see if the Martians were doing their jobs right. He'd order them about harshly.

"Go on! Hurry up! Grab that flat, you two. Not that way, you dope! *Right* side up, *right* side up!"

And they all kept running around like tiny deaf mutes, laboring at a hopeless task.

I looked around. But I couldn't see Larg. I went over to the man. He looked up. "No one's allowed back here."

"I'm from the *Globe*," I told him, showing my card. His face changed. He looked interested.

"Yeah?" he said. "How'd you like the show? Good, haah?"

I nodded. What else could I do?

"You give us a good writeup?" he asked.

"Maybe," I said, "If you'll let me look around back here. Maybe talk to a few of your—actors."

"What actors? Oh—them. What do you wanna talk to them for?" he asked.

"Don't they talk?" I asked.

He squinted. "Yeah," he admitted. As though he were telling me that, sure, the parrot could talk but you can't very well converse with it.

"Look," he said, "you wanna see Mr. Terwilliger? He can tell you anything you wanna know."

"I want to see Larg," I told him.

He looked at me curiously. "What for?"

"Just to talk to him."

He looked at me blankly. Then he shrugged his thick shoulders.

"Go ahead, buddy," he said, "if you wanna waste your time. Say you'll give us a good writeup?"

"Read the *Globe* tomorrow," I answered.

"Yeah, I'll do that," he said. "I'll just do that."

He pointed to his left. "The Marshie is back there in the dressing room."

"Doesn't he work?" I asked. All the other "Marshies" were working.

The man looked disgusted. "He's *s'posed* to work," he said. "But he's a goof-off. Thinks he's the star."

His voice went up to a squeak as he mimicked Larg. ' "I'm sick, I'm sick!' "

"I understand." I nodded.

I went back and stood by the door. Inside I could hear a faint flutter of coughing—like the coughing of a frail old woman.

I knocked.

The coughing increased. Then I heard him ask who it was.

"May I come in and speak to you?" I asked. "I'm from the *Globe*."

There was a long moment of silence. I stood there restlessly. Finally I heard him cough once more. Then he said, "I can't keep you out."

The room was very dimly lit. Larg was sitting on a shabby couch, his small oddly-proportioned body dwarfed the pillow he leaned on. He had his tubelike legs propped up before him.

He looked up as I came in. He didn't say anything—just looked. And then he lowered his eyes again. A cough rocked his small body.

I sat down on a chair across from him. I didn't speak. I kept watching him. He looked up finally. His eyes were yellow—and bitter. "Well?" he said.

His voice was pitched lower than it had been while he was portraying Rip Van Winkle.

I told him my name. I asked him how he was.

He looked at me clinically. I couldn't tell what he was thinking. His gaze was expressionless. A slight cough shook him. Then his pointed shoulders twitched back.

"Why should you care?" he asked.

I started to answer. But he interrupted.

"It's an interview you want, isn't it?" he said. "An interview with the funny little marionette. With the ugly, little yellow-eyed Martian."

"I didn't come to—"

"To be insulted?"

His voice was shrill again. He pushed himself back against the pillow and his small stubby nostrils flared out. Then he closed his eyes. Suddenly. His hands dropped in his lap.

"No, of course not," he said. "You want some pleasant little anecdote. Boy on Mars yearning for the theater life. The big chance—cheers—flowers—romance of the footlights. God bless Earth.''

He opened his eyes and looked at me. ''That's what you want' isn't it?'' he asked.

I was quiet for a moment. Then I said, ''I didn't come for an interview. I'm only supposed to write up the performance.''

''Then why are you here?'' he asked. ''Curiosity? Burning desire to goggle?''

''No,'' I said.

Then we sat in painful silence. I had no idea of what to say, I felt terribly ill at ease.

Not because I was alone with a strange extraterrestrial being. That wasn't it. I've seen enough pictures, enough shows, enough movies. The shock of appearances wears down quickly.

I'll tell you why I was shocked.

Because I was realizing more and more that this small ''creature,'' as you would call him, *wasn't* a mere creature.

He was not, as I had been brought up to believe, some subspecies of animal life with only gifts for mimicking other languages. Not at all. He was an intelligent person.

And he hated me. That's why I felt ill at ease. Because to be hated by an animal is nothing. But to be hated by a rational being is a lot.

''What do you want?'' he asked.

''I'd—like to talk to you.'' I hesitated.

He started to speak. But then a violent fit of coughing tore at his voice. His fragile hands shot out to grab a towel from the couch beside him.

He plunged his face into it. And I sat there watching his toothpick shoulders tremble. And hearing his pathetic gagging muffled in the towel, and the horrible coughing.

The coughing eased. He gasped for breath. There were tears shining in his eyes. ''Go away please,'' he said, his voice broken and humiliated. He avoided my gaze.

''You need a doctor,'' I said.

His chest shuddered again. It was laughter this time.

Laughter that had no amusement in it.

"You're very amusing," he wheezed. "Now will you leave me alone?"

I spoke impatiently—as we do when we do not understand. "Listen, I'm not trying to be funny. You're ill and you need a doctor."

The coughing stopped. He looked at me. "You don't understand," he said. "I'm a Martian."

"I don't see . . ."

"You're supposed to laugh at me!"

And I felt myself tighten with rage. No—not at him. The rage was for those far-flung generations that had taught me and my brothers to consider Martians as inferior stock.

Because here—in a split second—the entire lie had been flung into my teeth. And there is no more stunning and enraging shock than to have centuries of lies explode in your face.

He leaned weakly against the pillow, the towel held in his lap. I noticed that it was spotted with dark splotches. His blood. When he saw that I noticed, he quickly folded the towel so that only clean surfaces showed.

"Larg," I said, "if you feel up to it, will you tell me about yourself? And about your people?"

"For publication?" he asked, his tone slightly less cynical. "For an amusing froth in the Sunday supplement?"

I shook my head. "No, just for me."

He looked at me carefully. I couldn't tell whether he believed me or not. But I *could* still feel his shrinking, his distaste for me.

He said, "I suppose you saw my people working backstage."

I nodded. "Yes, I did."

He rubbed a hand over his pale lips. "They're like me," he said, "all sick. All exiles. Exiles of economy."

"I don't . . ."

He coughed once. "We're all here, you see, because we need the money."

"Can't you work on your own planet?"

He glanced at me as though he thought I joked. Then he shook his head. "No, there's nothing there," he said. "Nothing."

We sat in silence a moment. Once again he began to cough into the towel, his face coloring apoplectically. When the spasm had passed his breath came in tortured gasps.

"You'd better not speak any more," I said.

"Why not?" he said. "It doesn't make any difference."

"Are you married, Larg?" I asked.

He smiled bitterly at something I could not see. "I think so," he said. "I'm not sure—any more."

"When did you see your wife last?"

He looked down at his hands. Blankly. "Fifteen years ago," he said.

"*Fifteen!*"

"Yes."

"But—but why?"

"It's very simple," he said, the undercurrent of hate and resentment hard in his voice. "I was teacher of history at the Rakasa School, as you Earth people called it." He paused. "Before you tore it down," he said.

He leaned back his head and stared at the ceiling. "I needed work to support my wife and our children. I joined this company. Other men became miners in their own mines. Laborers, servants, slaves . . ."

He looked down at me. And it was as though his people looked with murderous hate upon ours. A hate time could never wipe out.

"The rest died," he said, "seven millions of them."

I sat there, numb with shock of his words. I just couldn't understand them, believe them.

For I, like you, had heard of these things, read distorted glossed-over reports on the decimation of the Martian race. Studied from history books that told of disease and drought and famine. Of internecine warfare, of savage death-attacks on Earth military posts on Mars. Of racial suicide due to psychotic pride.

The blame has always been displaced. Twisted, contorted,

dropped on the Martians, on Nature, on everything—except us. It is never placed on us.

Those were the thoughts I had. And through all my thinking I could hear the fragile flutter of Larg's breath. Like the last feeble protest of a murdered race.

And then, like a loyal Earthman, I would not even then accept the blame. "I never knew," I said. "I don't expect you'll believe me, but I never knew."

He sighed. "What does it matter?" he said.

Silence again. Nervously I took out my cigarettes. I offered him one. He shook his head. I noticed the bluish veins in his forehead. I lit the cigarette and blew a cloud of smoke to the side.

"Why do you do that?" he asked.

I don't understand. "Do what?" I asked.

"Blow the smoke away from me?"

I still didn't know. I shrugged. "I don't go around blowing smoke at people's faces," I said.

He stared at me for a long moment. Then something seemed to resolve itself in his expression. He relaxed back against the pillow. "So," he said, "I'm people."

He made a sound of tired amusement. "Why, I'd forgotten it," he said ironically.

And what could I say? Let me admit it—as we all should admit it. I was penitent and mute before this fellow-creature. Yes, *fellow*-creature, though we have not earned even the right to claim him as brother.

Does that shock you, reader? Does that offend your sensibilities? I can well imagine that it does.

For how should a man feel if he is told that what he has always regarded as inferior to him is equal? And, perhaps, *superior*. How should a man greet the news that his standards are wrong?

No, I expect little sympathy for this account. No man loves another who has shown his frailty to the light.

But I write anyway. For I, too, was one of you just this early evening. I, too, believed myself a liberal mind, thought that I had won my personal triumph over bigotry. I, too, felt perfectly justified in standing on the soapbox of the universe and crying—"I am of the clean, the pure in heart!"

Well, I was wrong. You see that. Or maybe you don't.

"What's your name, young man?" Larg asked.

Once again I felt shock. And yet it was obvious that he was no child, no mere cynical youth. He was much older than I and much wiser.

"My name?" I faltered. "Walter. Walter Thompson."

And I knew he would never forget it then. He nodded—and looked at me without rancor for the first time. "You know my name," he said quietly.

And the way he sait it, it was a gentle, unspoken invitation to friendship.

"Why did you come back here?" he asked.

I started to speak. But then I had to stop. Because I had no answer. "I don't know," I finally admitted, shaking my head. "I'm afraid I just don't know."

And for the first time, Larg smiled at me. "Well, that's a novelty," he said, his gentle voice bubbling with an undercurrent of kind amusement. "You're the first Earthman I ever met who admitted not knowing everything."

I tried to smile back. But, somehow, I couldn't. "I could give you any number of reasons why I didn't come back here," I said, "but for a reason I *did* . . . I'm stumped."

He sat up a little. His eyes became bright and interested. He cleared his throat delicately and put his hands on his kneecaps.

"I have found that to be commonplace among you Earth people," he said, "the ready knowledge of why you *don't* do things. But no attendant ability to explain why you *do* execute them."

He smiled again. And we both smiled, one at the other. As men smile when they are friends.

"If you would really like to interview me," he said, "I wouldn't mind. Not now."

Hurriedly I put out my cigarette in an ashtray. The outlines of a plan were rising in my mind.

"Listen, Larg," I said.

He listened.

"I'm no intellect," I said. "I haven't the ability to split hairs—or to delve into sociological aspects or philosophy or anything like that.

"But I *can* report. And this situation cries for reporting. I want to tell the readers about you. Not about Rip Van Winkle. Not about the funny little guy from Mars."

I felt my throat contract. "I don't think about you that way anymore," I said. "I think you're as good as the rest of..."

Then I twisted my shoulders impatient with my own words.

"I'm sorry," I said, "I don't mean to sound smug or self-righteous. Believe me, I'm ashamed—terribly ashamed. For myself and for my people. But I—I just don't know how to put it."

"You see, I've been brought up to believe the things I believed about you. That others still believe. And now that those beliefs have been pretty well kicked out from under me—well, I'm a little fuzzy at the edges."

Our eyes met. And I thought suddenly how differences in appearance disappear when you look at minds instead of faces.

Larg seemed a brother then. Not an Earth-brother or a Mars-brother. I mean a brother—a person possessing that nonracial, universal trait which is separate from feature or environment. That sense of being which may exist in the savage and not in the priest.

Or in the Martian and not in the Earthman. A dignity, a self-respect, a soul.

Larg looked at me, smiling. "You've said it very well," he said.

I put out my hand. Then I jerked it back. I wasn't sure. I started to speak to cover the move. And Larg said, "Yes, I'd *like* to shake your hand."

He extended his small fingers. I grasped them as gently as I could. Something beyond anything I had ever felt surged up in me. I can't explain it. But if it ever happens to you you'll know it.

We clasped hands for a long moment.

"I wish I could give you something more than words," I told him, "Something substantial. A doctor, a letter from your wife and children, a promise to get you home—anything. But I—I can't."

He smiled. "You've given me much," he said, "something more valuable than you may realize. For you have an excess of it each day, I'm sure."

He looked at me carefully. "You've given me friendship," he said, "understanding, respect."

Then he closed his eyes. His lips tightened. "Those are things that *we* must have as well as you," he said quietly; "those are things without which no being is complete."

When Walt came in the next morning the city editor called him in. He tossed the review across his desk.

"Finish this off," he said, "I started the deletions."

Walt asked, "What deletions?"

"Cut out all that stuff about the murder of a race. Larg and his noble character. Handle it straight. The show, the kids' reactions. That's all we want."

Walt looked at Barton in disbelief. "You're not going to run it?" he asked.

Barton's eyelids flickered. "You know our policy, Thompson. You knew damn well we couldn't run it."

"No, *I didn't*." Walt clenched his fists. "I thought this was a newspaper. Not somebody's propaganda sheet—not some rich man's solace."

Barton looked up at him like a harried father. "Where have you been, Walter?" he said patiently. "Welcome back to reality."

Walt tossed the review back on Barton's desk. "It goes like that or not at all," he snapped.

"Then not at all," Barton said. "Look, Walt, what are you jumping on me for? *I* don't make policy."

"You help it along!"

"Sit down, Walt," Barton said, gesturing.

Walt slumped down in the chair facing Barton's desk. The editor leaned back.

"I've been wondering how long it would take you to come up with something like this," he said. "It's been overdue. Usually you kids get it out of your system right after college. They don't let it linger inside them until they're married and have a kid like you."

Barton fingered the review.

"We *can't* run it, kid," he said. "You know that as well as I do. No matter how true it is."

"Then truth isn't the criterion any more," Walt said acidly.

"Was it ever?" Barton said. "We killed it. The same way I'll have to kill your review unless you doctor it. Let's be practical about this."

"Practical!"

They stared at each other.

"Is it an order?" Walt asked. "Am I ordered to cut its heart out?"

Barton shrugged. "Call it an order then," he said. "Pin it on me if it will make you feel any better."

Walt's face tightened. "Sure," he said, "that will make me feel just fine."

Barton sighed. "Well, here it is, Walt. It's out of my hands, it's policy."

"Policy!" Walt jumped to his feet. "God damn the word!"

They were silent. Barton held out the review. Walt didn't budge.

"I know how you feel, Walter," Barton said, "but you're in a trap, don't you see? *I'm* in a trap. We all are. And we can't afford to tear ourselves loose."

Walt took the review.

"I know what you're going through," said Barton.

"No, you don't," Walt said very quietly, "not any more." He turned at the door. "And some day," he said, "I'll be just like you."

He rewrote the story. He cut, chiseled, reworded. It

emerged from his efforts clean and pleasant and without subversion. He sent it downstairs and it was printed.

That night he read it as he rode home on the pneumatic tube. He thought about Larg reading it. First anxiously, then with rising disappointment. Then at last with desparing bitterness.

They would never see each other again.

He crumpled the paper and threw it down a disposal chute as he got off the tube car. "He thinks *he* has troubles," he muttered angrily as he walked home.

He thought of the red tape involved in leaving one job and getting another. It took the Position Bureau at least six months. And in the meantime there were bills to be paid. He thought of them. Food bills, clothing bills, payments on the ground-car and the house and the furniture and everything.

He almost hated Larg for injecting dissatisfaction into his life.

Then, after supper, he sat in his clean bright living room and thought of it again. Full circle, he thought. That was what it amounted to.

Larg couldn't do anything about it. *He* couldn't do anything about it. Both of them, knowing the situation for what it was, were powerless to change it. They were hemmed in. Bound within an enchanted circle of economics, of policy.

"What's the matter?" asked his wife that night.

"I'm sick, that's what's the matter," he said. "I'm very damned sick."

# Nightmare at 20,000 Feet

"Seat belt, please," said the stewardess cheerfully as she passed him.

Almost as she spoke, the sign above the archway which led to the forward compartment lit up—FASTEN SEAT BELT—with, below its attendant caution—NO SMOKING. Drawing in a deep lungful, Wilson exhaled it in bursts, then pressed the cigarette into the arm rest tray with irritable stabbing motions.

Outside, one of the engines coughed monstrously, spewing out a cloud of fume which fragmented into the night air. The fuselage began to shudder and Wilson, glancing through the window, saw the exhaust of flame jetting whitely from the engine's nacelle. The second engine coughed, then roared, its propeller instantly a blur of revolution. With a tense submissiveness, Wilson fastened the belt across his lap.

Now all the engines were running and Wilson's head throbbed in unison with the fuselage. He sat rigidly, staring at the seat ahead as the DC-7 taxied across the apron, heating the night with the thundering blast of its exhausts.

At the edge of the runway, it halted. Wilson looked out through the window at the leviathan glitter of the terminal. By late morning, he thought, showered and cleanly dressed, he would be sitting in the office of one more contact discussing one more specious deal, the net result of which would not add one jot of meaning to the history of mankind. It was all so damned—

Wilson gasped as the engines began their warm-up race preparatory to takeoff. The sound, already loud, became deafening—waves of sound that crashed against Wilson's ears like club blows. He opened his mouth as if to let it drain. His eyes took on the glaze of a suffering man, his hands drew in like tensing claws.

He started, legs retracting, as he felt a touch on his arm. Jerking aside his head, he saw the stewardess who had met him at the door. She was smiling down at him.

"Are you all right?" he barely made out her words.

Wilson pressed his lips together and agitated his hand at her as if pushing her away. Her smile flared into excess brightness, then fell as she turned and moved away.

The plane began to move. At first lethargically, like some behemoth struggling to overthrow the pull of its own weight. Then with more speed, forcing off the drag of friction. Wilson, turning to the window, saw the dark runway rushing by faster and faster. On the wing edge, there was a mechanical whining as the flaps descended. Then, imperceptibly, the giant wheels lost contact with the ground, the earth began to fall away. Trees flashed underneath, buildings, the darting quicksilver of car lights. The DC-7 banked slowly to the right, pulling itself upward toward the frosty glitter of the stars.

Finally, it levelled off and the engines seemed to stop until Wilson's adjusting ear caught the murmur of their cruising speed. A moment of relief slackened his muscles, imparting a sense of well-being. Then it was gone. Wilson sat immobile, staring at the NO SMOKING sign until it winked out, then, quickly, lit a cigarette. Reaching into the seat-back pocket in front of him, he slid free his newspaper.

As usual, the world was in a state similar to his. Friction in diplomatic circles, earthquakes and gunfire, murder, rape, tornadoes and collisions, business conflicts, gangsterism. God's in his heaven, all's right with the world, thought Arthur Jeffrey Wilson.

Fifteen minutes later, he tossed the paper aside. His stomach felt awful. He glanced up at the signs beside the two lavatories. Both, illuminated, read OCCUPIED. He pressed out his third cigarette since takeoff and, turning off the overhead light, stared out through the window.

Along the cabin's length, people were already flicking out their lights and reclining their chairs for sleep. Wilson glanced at his watch. Eleven-twenty. He blew out tired breath. As he'd anticipated, the pills he'd taken before boarding hadn't done a bit of good.

He stood abruptly as the woman came out of the lavatory and, snatching up his bag, started down the aisle.

His system, as expected, gave no cooperation. Wilson stood with a tired moan and adjusted his clothing. Having washed his hands and face, he removed the toilet kit from the bag and squeezed a filament of paste across his toothbrush.

As he brushed, one hand braced for support against the cold bulkhead, he looked out through the port. Feet away was the pale blue of the inboard propeller. Wilson visualized what would happen if it were to tear loose and, like a tribladed cleaver, come slicing in at him.

There was a sudden depression in his stomach. Wilson swallowed instinctively and got some paste-stained saliva down his throat. Gagging, he turned and spat into the sink, then, hastily, washed out his mouth and took a drink. Dear God, if only he could have gone by train; had his own compartment, taken a casual stroll to the club car, settled down in an easy chair with a drink and a magazine. But there was no such time or fortune in this world.

He was about to put the toilet kit away when his gaze caught on the oilskin envelope in the bag. He hesitated, then, setting the small briefcase on the sink, drew out the envelope and undid it on his lap.

He sat staring at the oil-glossed symmetry of the pistol. He'd carried it around with him for almost a year now. Originally, when he'd thought about it, it was in terms of money carried, protection from holdup, safety from teenage gangs in the cities he had to attend. Yet, far beneath, he'd always known there was no valid reason except one. A reason he thought more of every day. How simple it would be—here, now—

Wilson shut his eyes and swallowed quickly. He could still

taste the toothpaste in his mouth, a faint nettling of peppermint on the buds. He sat heavily in the throbbing chill of the lavatory, the oily gun resting in his hands. Until, quite suddenly, he began to shiver without control. God, let me go! his mind cried out abruptly.

"Let me go, *let me go*." He barely recognized the whimpering in his ears.

Abruptly, Wilson sat erect. Lips pressed together, he rewrapped the pistol and thrust it into his bag, putting the briefcase on top of it, zipping the bag shut. Standing, he opened the door and stepped outside, hurrying to his seat and sitting down, sliding the overnight bag precisely into place. He indented the armrest button and pushed himself back. He was a business man and there was business to be conducted on the morrow. It was as simple as that. The body needed sleep, he would give it sleep.

Twenty minutes later, Wilson reached down slowly and depressed the button, sitting up with the chair, his face a mask of vanquished acceptance. Why fight it? he thought. It was obvious he was going to stay awake. So that was that.

He had finished half of the crossword puzzle before he let the paper drop to his lap. His eyes were too tired. Sitting up, he rotated his shoulders, stretching the muscles of his back. Now what? he thought. He didn't want to read, he couldn't sleep. And there were still—he checked his watch—seven to eight hours left before Los Angeles was reached. How was he to spend them? He looked along the cabin and saw that, except for a single passenger in the forward compartment, everyone was asleep.

A sudden, overwhelming fury filled him and he wanted to scream, to throw something, to hit somebody. Teeth jammed together so rabidly it hurt his jaws. Wilson shoved aside the curtains with a spastic hand and stared out murderously through the window.

Outside, he saw the wing lights blinking off and on, the lurid flashes of exhaust from the engine cowlings. Here he was, he thought; twenty thousand feet above the earth, trapped in a howling shell of death, moving through polar night toward—

Wilson twitched as lightning bleached the sky, washing its false daylight across the wing. He swallowed. Was there going to be a storm? The thought of rain and heavy winds, of the plane a chip in a sea of sky was not a pleasant one. Wilson was a bad flyer. Excess motion always made him ill. Maybe he should have taken another few Dramamine pills to be on the safe side. And, naturally, his seat was next to the emergency door. He thought about it opening accidentally; about himself sucked from the plane, falling, screaming.

Wilson blinked and shook his head. There was a faint tingling at the back of his neck as he pressed close to the window and stared out. He sat there motionless, squinting. He could have sworn—

Suddenly, his stomach muscles jerked in violently and he felt his eyes strain forward. There was something crawling on the wing.

Wilson felt a sudden, nauseous tremor in his stomach. Dear God, had some dog or cat crawled onto the plane before takeoff and, in some way managed to hold on? It was a sickening thought. The poor animal would be deranged with terror. Yet, how, on the smooth, wind-blasted surface, could it possibly discover gripping places? Surely that was impossible. Perhaps, after all, it was only a bird or—

The lightning flared and Wilson saw that it was a man.

He couldn't move. Stupefied, he watched the black form crawling down the wing. *Impossible*. Somewhere, cased in layers of shock, a voice declared itself but Wilson did not hear. He was conscious of nothing but the titanic, almost muscle-tearing leap of his heart—and of the man outside.

Suddenly, like ice-filled water thrown across him, there was a reaction; his mind sprang for the shelter of explanation. A mechanic had, through some incredible oversight, been taken up with the ship and had managed to cling to it even though the wind had torn his clothes away, even though the air was thin and close to freezing.

Wilson gave himself no time for refutation. Jarring to his

feet, he shouted: "Stewardess! Stewardess!" his voice a hollow, ringing sound in the cabin. He pushed the button for her with a jabbing finger.

"*Stewardess!*"

She came running down the aisle, her face tightened with alarm. When she saw the look on his face, she stiffened in her tracks.

"There's a man out there! A man!" cried Wilson.

"*What?*" Skin constricted on her cheeks, around her eyes.

"Look, *look!*" Hand shaking, Wilson dropped back into his seat and pointed out the window. "He's crawling on the—"

The words ended with a choking rattle in his throat. There was nothing on the wing.

Wilson sat there trembling. For a while, before he turned back, he looked at the reflection of the stewardess on the window. There was a blank expression on her face.

At last, he turned and looked up at her. He saw her red lips part as though she meant to speak but she said nothing, only placing the lips together again and swallowing. An attempted smile distended briefly at her features.

"I'm sorry," Wilson said. "It must have been a—"

He stopped as though the sentence were completed. Across the aisle a teenage girl was gaping at him with sleepy curiosity.

The stewardess cleared her throat. "Can I get you anything?" she asked.

"A glass of water," Wilson said.

The stewardess turned and moved back up the aisle.

Wilson sucked in a long breath of air and turned away from the young girl's scrutiny. He felt the same. That was the thing that shocked him most. Where were the visions, the cries, the pummelling of fists on temples, the tearing out of hair?

Abruptly he closed his eyes. There had been a man, he thought. There had, actually, been a man. That's why he felt the same. And yet, there couldn't have been. He knew that clearly.

Wilson sat with his eyes closed, wondering what Jacqueline would be doing now if she were in the seat beside him. Would she be silent, shocked beyond speaking? Or would she, in the more accepted manner, be fluttering around him, smiling, chattering, pretending that she hadn't seen? What would his sons think? Wilson felt a dry sob threatening in his chest. Oh, God—

"Here's your water, sir."

Twitching sharply, Wilson opened his eyes.

"Would you like a blanket?" inquired the stewardess.

"No." He shook his head. "Thank you," he added, wondering why he was being so polite.

"If you need anything, just ring," she said.

Wilson nodded.

Behind him, as he sat with the untouched cup of water in his hand, he heard the muted voices of the stewardess and one of the passengers. Wilson tightened with resentment. Abruptly, he reached down and, careful not to spill the water, pulled out the overnight bag. Unzipping it, he removed the box of sleeping capsules and washed two of them down. Crumpling the empty cup, he pushed it into the seat-pocket in front of him, then, not looking, slid the curtains shut. There—it was ended. One hallucination didn't make insanity.

Wilson turned onto his right side and tried to set himself against the fitful motion of the ship. He had to forget about this, that was the most important thing. He mustn't dwell on it. Unexpectedly, he found a wry smile forming on his lips. Well, by God, no one could accuse him of mundane hallucinations anyway. When he went at it, he did a royal job. A naked man crawling down a DC-7's wing at twenty thousand feet—there was a chimera worthy of the noblest lunatic.

The humor faded quickly. Wilson felt chilled. It had been so clear, so vivid. How could the eyes see such a thing when it did not exist? How could what was in his mind make the physical act of seeing work to its purpose so completely? He hadn't been groggy, in a daze—nor had it been a shapeless, gauzy vision. It had been sharply three-dimensional, fully a part of the things he saw which he *knew* were real. That was the frightening part of it. It had not been dreamlike in the least. He had looked at the wing and—

Impulsively, Wilson drew aside the curtain.

He did not know, immediately, if he would survive. It seemed as if all the contents of his chest and stomach were bloating horribly, the excess pushing up into his throat and head, choking away breath, pressing out his eyes. Imprisoned in this swollen mass, his heart pulsed strickenly, threatening to burst its case as Wilson sat, paralyzed.

Only inches away; separated from him by the thickness of a piece of glass, the man was staring at him.

It was a hideously malignant face, a face not human. Its skin was grimy, of a wide-pored coarseness; its nose a squat, discolored lump; its lips misshapen, cracked, forced apart by teeth of a grotesque size and crookedness; its eyes recessed and small—unblinking. All framed by shaggy, tangled hair which sprouted, too, in furry tufts from the man's ears and nose, in birdlike down across his cheeks.

Wilson sat riven to his chair, incapable of response. Time stopped and lost its meaning. Function and analysis ceased. All were frozen in an ice of shock. Only the beat of heart went on—alone, a frantic leaping in the darkness. Wilson could not so much as blink. Dull-eyed, breathless, he returned the creature's vacant stare.

Abruptly then, he closed his eyes and his mind, rid of the sight, broke free. It isn't there, he thought. He pressed his teeth together, breath quavering in his nostrils. It isn't there, *it simply is not there*.

Clutching at the arm rests with pale-knuckled fingers, Wilson braced himself. There is no man out there, he told himself. It was impossible that there should be a man out there crouching on the wing looking at him.

He opened his eyes—

—to shrink against the seat back with a gagging inhalation. Not only was the man still there but he was grinning. Wilson turned his fingers in and dug the nails into his palms until pain flared. He kept it there until there was no doubt in his mind that he was fully conscious.

Then, slowly, arm quivering and numb, Wilson reached

up for the button which would summon the stewardess. He would not make the same mistake again—cry out, leap to his feet, alarm the creature into flight. He kept reaching upward, a tremor of aghast excitement in his muscles now because the man was watching him, the small eyes shifting with the movement of his arm.

He pressed the button carefully once, twice. Now come, he thought. Come with your objective eyes and see what I see—but *hurry*.

In the rear of the cabin, he heard a curtain being drawn aside and, suddenly, his body stiffened. The man had turned his caliban head to look in that direction. Paralyzed, Wilson stared at him. Hurry, he thought. For God's sake, hurry!

It was over in a second. The man's eyes shifted back to Wilson, across his lips a smile of monstrous cunning. Then with a leap, he was gone.

"Yes, sir?"

For a moment, Wilson suffered the fullest anguish of madness. His gaze kept jumping from the spot where the man had stood to the stewardess's questioning face, then back again. Back to the stewardess, to the wing, to the stewardess, his breath caught, his eyes stark with dismay.

"What *is* it?" asked the stewardess.

It was the look on her face that did it. Wilson closed a vise on his emotions. She couldn't possibly believe him. He realized it in an instant.

"I'm—I'm sorry," he faltered. He swallowed so dryly that it made a clicking noise in his throat. "It's nothing. I—apologize."

The stewardess obviously didn't know what to say. She kept leaning against the erratic yawing of the ship, one hand holding on to the back of the seat beside Wilson's, the other stirring limply along the seam of her skirt. Her lips were parted slightly as if she meant to speak but could not find the words.

"Well," she said finally and cleared her throat, "if you—need anything."

"Yes, yes. Thank you. Are we—going into a storm?"

The stewardess smiled hastily. "Just a small one," she said. "Nothing to worry about."

Wilson nodded with little twitching movements. Then, as the stewardess turned away, breathed in suddenly, his nostrils flaring. He felt certain that she already thought him mad but didn't know what to do about it because, in her course of training, there had been no instruction on the handling of passengers who thought they saw small men crouching on the wing.

*Thought?*

Wilson turned his head abruptly and looked outside. He stared at the dark rise of the wing, the spouting flare of the exhausts, the blinking lights. He's *seen* the man—to that he'd swear. How could he be completely aware of everything around him—be, in all ways, sane and still imagine such a thing? Was it logical that the mind, in giving way, should, instead of distorting all reality, insert within the still intact arrangement of details, one extraneous sight?

No, not logical at all.

Suddenly, Wilson thought about war, about the newspaper stories which recounted the alleged existence of creatures in the sky who plagued the Allied pilots in their duties. They called them gremlins, he remembered. Were there, actually, such beings? Did they, truly, exist up here, never falling, riding on the wind, apparently of bulk and weight, yet impervious to gravity?

He was thinking that when the man appeared again.

One second the wing was empty. The next, with an arcing descent, the man came jumping down to it. There seemed no impact. He landed almost fragilely, short, hairy arms outstretched as if for balance. Wilson tensed. Yes, there was knowledge in his look. The man—was he to think of it as a man?—somehow understood that he had tricked Wilson into calling the stewardess in vain. Wilson felt himself tremble with alarm. How could he prove the man's existence to others? He looked around desperately. That girl across the aisle. If he spoke to her softly, woke her up, would she be able to—

No, the man would jump away before she could see. Probably to the top of the fuselage where no one could see him, not even the pilots in their cockpit. Wilson felt a sudden burst of self-condemnation that he hadn't gotten that camera Walter had asked for. Dear Lord, he thought, to be able to take a picture of the man.

He leaned in close to the window. What was the man doing?

Abruptly, darkness seemed to leap away as the wing was chalked with lightning and Wilson saw. Like an inquisitive child, the man was squatted on the hitching wing edge, stretching out his right hand toward one of the whirling propellers.

As Wilson watched, fascinatedly appalled, the man's hand drew closer and closer to the blurring gyre until, suddenly, it jerked away and the man's lips twitched back in a soundless cry. He's lost a finger! Wilson thought, sickened. But, immediately, the man reached forward again, gnarled finger extended, the picture of some monstrous infant trying to capture the spin of a fan blade.

If it had not been so hideously out of place it would have been amusing for, objectively seen, the man, at that moment, was a comic sight—a fairy tale troll somehow come to life, wind whipping at the hair across his head and body, all of his attention centered on the turn of the propeller. How could this be madness? Wilson suddenly thought. What self-revelation could this farcical little horror possibly bestow on him?

Again and again, as Wilson watched, the man reached forward. Again and again jerked back his fingers, sometimes, actually, putting them in his mouth as if to cool them. And, always, apparently checking, he kept glancing back across at his shoulder looking at Wilson. *He knows*, thought Wilson. Knows that this is a game between us. If I am able to get someone else to see him, then he loses. If I am the only witness, then he wins. The sense of faint amusement was gone now. Wilson clenched his teeth. Why in hell didn't the pilots see!

Now the man, no longer interested in the propeller, was

settling himself across the engine cowling like a man astride a bucking horse. Wilson stared at him. Abruptly a shudder plaited down his back. The little man was picking at the plates that sheathed the engine, trying to get his nails beneath them.

Impulsively, Wilson reached up and pushed the button for the stewardess. In the rear of the cabin, he heard her coming and, for a second, thought he'd fooled the man, who seemed absorbed with his efforts. At the last moment, however, just before the stewardess arrived, the man glanced over at Wilson. Then, like a marionette jerked upward from its stage by wires, he was flying up into the air.

"Yes?" She looked at him apprehensively.

"Will you—sit down, please?" he asked.

She hesitated. "Well, I—"

"Please."

She sat down gingerly on the seat beside his.

"What is it, Mr. Wilson?" she asked.

He braced himself.

"That man is still outside," he said.

The stewardess stared at him.

"The reason I'm telling you this," Wilson hurried on, "is that he's starting to tamper with one of the engines."

She turned her eyes instinctively toward the window.

"No, no, don't look," he told her. "He isn't there now." He cleared his throat viscidly. "He—jumps away whenever you come here."

A sudden nausea gripped him as he realized what she must be thinking. As he realized what he, himself, would think if someone told him such a story. A wave of dizziness seemed to pass across him and he thought—I *am* going mad!

"The point is this," he said, fighting off the thought. "If I'm not imagining this thing, the ship is in danger."

"Yes," she said.

"I know," he said. "You think I've lost my mind."

"Of course not," she said.

"All I ask is this," he said, struggling against the rise of anger. "Tell the pilots what I've said. Ask them to keep an eye on the wings. If they see nothing—all right. But if they do—"

The stewardess sat there quietly, looking at him. Wilson's hands curled into fists that trembled in his lap.

"*Well?*" he asked.

She pushed to her feet. "I'll tell them," she said.

Turning away, she moved along the aisle with a movement that was, to Wilson, poorly contrived—too fast to be normal yet, clearly, held back as if to reassure him that she wasn't fleeing. He felt his stomach churning as he looked out at the wing again.

Abruptly, the man appeared again, landing on the wing like some grotesque ballet dancer. Wilson watched him as he set to work again, straddling the engine casing with his thick, bare legs and picking at the plates.

Well, what was he so concerned about? thought Wilson. That miserable creature couldn't pry up rivets with his fingernails. Actually, it didn't matter if the pilots saw him or not—at least so far as the safety of the plane was concerned. As for his own personal reasons—

It was at that moment that the man pried up one edge of a plate.

Wilson gasped. "Here, quickly!" he shouted, noticing, up ahead, the stewardess and the pilot coming through the cockpit doorway.

The pilot's eyes jerked up to look at Wilson, then abruptly, he was pushing past the stewardess and lurching up the aisle.

"*Hurry!*" Wilson cried. He glanced out the window in time to see the man go leaping upward. That didn't matter now. There would be evidence.

"What's going on?" the pilot asked, stopping breathlessly beside his seat.

"He's torn up one of the engine plates!" said Wilson in a shaking voice.

"He's what?"

"The man outside!" said Wilson. "I tell you he's—!"

"Mister Wilson, keep your voice down!" ordered the pilot.

Wilson's jaw went slack.

"I don't know what's going on here," said the pilot, "but—"

"Will you look?" shouted Wilson.

"Mister Wilson, I'm warning you."

"For God's sake!" Wilson swallowed quickly, trying to repress the blinding rage he felt. Abruptly, he pushed back against his seat and pointed at the window with a palsied hand. "Will you, for God's sake, *look?*" he asked.

Drawing in an agitated breath, the pilot bent over. In a moment, his gaze shifted coldly to Wilson's. "Well?" he asked.

Wilson jerked his head around. The plates were in their normal position.

"Oh, now wait," he said before the dread could come. "I saw him pry that plate up."

"Mister Wilson, if you don't—"

"*I said I saw him pry it up*," said Wilson.

The pilot stood there looking at him in the same withdrawn, almost aghast way as the stewardess had. Wilson shuddered violently.

"Listen, I *saw* him!" he cried. The sudden break in his voice appalled him.

In a second, the pilot was down beside him. "Mister Wilson, please," he said. "All right, you saw him. But remember there are other people aboard. We mustn't alarm them."

Wilson was too shaken to understand at first.

"You—mean you've *seen* him then?" he asked.

"Of course," the pilot said, "but we don't want to frighten the passengers. You can understand that."

"Of course, of course. I don't want to—"

Wilson felt a spastic coiling in his groin and lower stomach. Suddenly, he pressed his lips together and looked at the pilot with malevolent eyes.

"I understand," he said.

"The thing we have to remember—" began the pilot

"You can stop now," Wilson said.

"Sir?"

Wilson shuddered. "Get out of here," he said.

"Mr. Wilson, what—?"

"*Will you stop?*" Face whitening, Wilson turned from the pilot and stared out at the wing, eyes like stone.

He glared back suddenly.

"Rest assured I'll not say another word!" he snapped.

"Mr. Wilson, try to understand our—"

Wilson twisted away and stared out venomously at the engine. From a corner of vision, he saw two passengers standing in the aisle looking at him. *Idiots!* his mind exploded. He felt his hands begin to tremble and, for a few seconds, was afraid that he was going to vomit. It's the motion, he told himself. The plane was bucking in the air now like a storm-tossed boat.

He realized that the pilot was still talking to him and, refocusing his eyes, he looked at the man's reflection in the window. Beside him, mutely somber, stood the stewardess. Blind idiots, both of them, thought Wilson. He did not indicate his notice of their departure. Reflected on the window, he saw them heading toward the rear of the cabin. They'll be discussing me now, he thought. Setting up plans in case I grow violent.

He wished now that the man would reappear, pull off the cowling plate and ruin the engine. It gave him a sense of vengeful pleasure to know that only he stood between catastrophe and the more than thirty people aboard. If he chose, he could allow that catastrophe to take place. Wilson smiled without humor. There would be a royal suicide, he thought.

The little man dropped down again and Wilson saw that what he'd thought was correct—the man had pressed the plate back into place before jumping away. For, now, he was prying it up again and it was raising easily, peeling back like skin excised by some grotesque surgeon. The motion of the wing was very broken but the man seemed to have no difficulty staying balanced.

Once more Wilson felt panic. What was he to do? No one believed him. If he tried to convince them any more they'd probably restrain him by force. If he asked the stewardess to sit by him it would be, at best, only a momentary reprieve. The second she departed or, remaining, fell asleep, the man would return. Even if she stayed awake beside him, what was to keep the man from tampering with the engines on the other wing? Wilson shuddered, a coldness of dread misting along his bones.

*Dear God, there was nothing to be done.*

He twitched as, across the window through which he watched the little man, the pilot's reflection passed. The insanity of the moment almost broke him—the man and the pilot within feet of each other, both seen by him yet not aware of one another. No, that was wrong. The little man had glanced across his shoulder as the pilot passed. As if he knew there was no need to leap off any more, that Wilson's capacity for interfering was at an end. Wilson suddenly trembled with mind-searing rage. I'll kill you! he thought! You filthy little animal, I'll *kill* you!

Outside, the engine faltered.

It lasted only for a second, but, in that second, it seemed to Wilson as if his heart had, also, stopped. He pressed against the window, staring. The man had bent the cowling plate far back and now was on his knees, poking a curious hand into the engine.

"Don't" Wilson heard the whimper of his own voice begging. "*Don't . . .*"

Again, the engine failed. Wilson looked around in horror. Was everyone deaf? He raised his hand to press the button for the stewardess, then jerked it back. No, they'd lock him up, restrain him somehow. And he was the only one who knew what was happening, the only one who could help.

"*God . . .*" Wilson bit his lower lip until the pain made him whimper. He twisted around again and jolted. The stewardess was hurrying down the rocking aisle. She'd heard it! He watched her fixedly and saw her glance at him as she passed his seat.

She stopped three seats down the aisle. Someone else had heard! Wilson watched the stewardess as she leaned over, talking to the unseen passenger. Outside, the engine coughed again. Wilson jerked his head around and looked out with horror-pinched eyes.

"*Damn you!*" he whined.

He turned again and saw the stewardess coming back up the aisle. She didn't look alarmed. Wilson stared at her with unbelieving eyes. It wasn't possible. He twisted around to follow her swaying movement and saw her turn in at the kitchen.

"*No.*" Wilson was shaking so badly now he couldn't stop. No one had heard.

No one knew.

Suddenly, Wilson bent over and slid his overnight bag out from under the seat. Unzipping it, he jerked out his briefcase and threw it on the carpeting. Then, reaching in again, he grabbed the oilskin envelope and straightened up. From the corners of his eyes, he saw the stewardess coming back and pushed the bag beneath the seat with his shoes, shoving the oilskin envelope beside himself. He sat there rigidly, breath quavering in his chest, as she went by.

Then he pulled the envelope into his lap and untied it. His movements were so feverish that he almost dropped the pistol. He caught it by the barrel, then clutched at the stock with white-knuckled fingers and pushed off the safety catch. He glanced outside and felt himself grow cold.

The man was looking at him.

Wilson pressed his shaking lips together. It was impossible that the man knew what he intended. He swallowed and tried to catch his breath. He shifted his gaze to where the stewardess was handing some pills to the passenger ahead, then looked back at the wing. The man was turning to the engine once again, reaching in. Wilson's grip tightened on the pistol. He began to raise it.

Suddenly, he lowered it. The window was too thick. The bullet might be deflected and kill one of the passengers. He shuddered and stared out at the little man. Again the engine failed and Wilson saw an eruption of sparks cast light across the man's animal features. He braced himself. There was only one answer.

He looked down at the handle of the emergency door. There was a transparent cover over it. Wilson pulled it free and dropped it. He looked outside. The man was still there, crouched and probing at the engine with his hand. Wilson sucked in trembling breath. He put his left hand on the door handle and tested. It wouldn't move downward. Upward there was play.

Abruptly, Wilson let go and put the pistol in his lap. No time for argument, he told himself. With shaking hands, he buckled the belt across his thighs. When the door was opened, there would be a tremendous rushing out of air. For the safety of the ship, he must not go with it.

Now. Wilson picked the pistol up again, his heartbeat staggering. He'd have to be sudden, accurate. If he missed, the man might jump onto the other wing—worse, onto the tail assembly where, inviolate, he could rupture wires, mangle flaps, destroy the balance of the ship. No, this was the only way. He'd fire low and try to hit the man in the chest or stomach. Wilson filled his lungs with air. Now, he thought. *Now.*

The stewardess came up the aisle as Wilson started pulling at the handle. For a moment, frozen in her steps, she couldn't speak. A look of stupified horror distended her features and she raised one hand as if imploring him. Then, suddenly, her voice was shrilling above the noise of the engines.

"*Mr. Wilson, no!*"

"Get back!" cried Wilson and he wrenched the handle up.

The door seemed to disappear. One second it was by him, in his grip. The next, with a hissing roar, it was gone.

In the same instant, Wilson felt himself enveloped by a monstrous suction which tried to tear him from his seat. His head and shoulders left the cabin and, suddenly, he was breathing tenuous, freezing air. For a moment, eardrums almost bursting from the thunder of the engines, eyes blinded by the arctic winds, he forgot the man. It seemed he heard a prick of screaming in the maelstrom that surrounded him, a distant shout.

Then Wilson saw the man.

He was walking across the wing, gnarled form leaning forward, talon-twisted hands outstretched in eagerness. Wilson flung his arm up, fired. The explosion was like a popping in the roaring violence of the air. The man staggered, lashed out and Wilson felt a streak of pain across his head. He fired again at immediate range and saw the man go flailing backward—then, suddenly, disappear with no more solidity than a paper doll swept in a gale. Wilson felt a bursting numbness in his brain. He felt the pistol torn from failing fingers.

Then all was lost in winter darkness.

He stirred and mumbled. There was a warmness trickling in his veins, his limbs felt wooden. In the darkness, he could hear a shuffling sound, a delicate swirl of voices. He was lying, face up, on something—moving, joggling. A cold wind sprinkled on his face, he felt the surface tilt beneath him.

He sighed. The plane was landed and he was being carried off on a stretcher. His head wound, likely, plus an injection to quiet him.

"Nuttiest way of tryin' to commit suicide *I* ever heard of," said a voice somewhere.

Wilson felt the pleasure of amusement. Whoever spoke was wrong, of course. As would be established soon enough when the engine was examined and they checked his wound more closely. Then they'd realize that he'd saved them all.

Wilson slept without dreams.